A BRUSH WITH DEATH

ROSIE MELEADY

ENVY PUBLISHING

To Dad

For inspiring me with stories such as The Chocolate Car and The Sad Daisy

BEFORE YOU START...

For updates, giveaways and insider clues to the next book, join Rosie Meleady's Cozy Book Crew on Facebook. The link is on my website: www.rosiemeleady.com

All characters and events in this series are fictional.

Social media: @ARosieLifeInItaly

Many thanks to Suzy Pope for her editing skills and Marco Marella for the cover design.

❦ Created with Vellum

1

"**I**'m pregnant."

"Are you sure?"

"Yes, I'm definite. I'm three months already, so I know it's not a severe case of gas," the tentative girlish voice down the phone line said.

"No, I mean definite about cancelling the wedding... a date at that venue is difficult to get and with only two months to go..." I could really do without another of the coming season's weddings postponed to the following year.

"I thought I'd get away with it, that no one would notice and I could go ahead with the date... but it's twins and I'm already as big as a bus." She giggled.

I checked her Instagram and saw a post captioned "12 weeks" with a selfie in a mirror. She looked gorgeous, glowing, her hand on her slight bump, the other holding the phone. I looked ten times more pregnant than her, although there was no hope of me being pregnant in my hot-flash, peri-menopausal state, and not having had time for a relationship in the last ten years.

"I'd never fit into my Channel dress, and I don't care how many hours in the gym or what diet I have to do, I will fit into again once the babies are born. I will have my day in that dress. I'm not cancelling, I just want to postpone to next year."

It was understandable why she wanted to wait. She had sent me a photo of the stunning dress. A uniquely patterned, frosted all over embroidered streamline design with a sheer train and deep-v neckline. It would give anyone all the motivation they needed to work off the baby pounds.

"She is the third bride to postpone this year due to a touch of pregnancy," I exclaimed down the phone to Paolo, my very attractive Italian man friend, who happened to call directly after her. "In all my 20 years of planning over 600 weddings, I've only had one bride get pregnant a few of months before the wedding, and she didn't cancel she went ahead with it. There's something weird about this year's season. It's like the gods know it's my last year doing weddings and have decided to throw everything at me. The bride, whose wedding was supposed to be next week, cancelled only two weeks ago her reason being 'she was a bit pregnant'. What's that supposed to mean?"

The other bride who told me about her impending bundle of blubbering joy, had the postponement discussion with me six months previous but it was too late for me to fill the date with a new client.

I had plenty of potential couples ready to jump into the cancelled date, but for me the rush of planning a destination wedding to Italy in six months rather than a full year was not worth the stress. I worked as a wedding planner because of my passion for logistics and detail, not for the money.

After so many years of weddings and teaching the art of wedding planning, I was comfortable financially. So much so that I had decided I would take early retirement the following year to enjoy developing my garden and renovating Brigid Borgo–my much-loved villa perched on the shore of Lake Trasimeno which I'd bought three years ago.

Paolo was laughing. "The postponements will mean you have some time off this summer, is that not a good thing?"

"No, once I put my wedding hat on, I like to stay in the zone."

"You have a wedding hat?"

"No, it's a saying." I often confuse Paolo when talking in my bad Italian. After three years of living in Italy, I was still not as fluent as I would have liked. My assistant, Sophia, once told me I talk like Yoda. "To shopping I like to go," is an example of some of the direct translations from my Italian efforts.

Even though Paolo could speak very good English, I liked to try to speak Italian with him as much as possible. 'When in Rome', as the saying goes. But let's not mention Rome... It was the first wedding of the season, and where I met up with Paolo again. I've had ten weddings since, and some sort of incident had happened at all of them ... but nothing like Rome. In Rome there was a murder, but that is a story for another time.

Paolo happened to be the manager at the wedding venue, and it was the first time our paths had crossed since our last steamy fling at a wedding industry conference four years previously. We had lost touch over the years. And, in that time, I had moved from Ireland to Italy. Not because I fell in love with him. That didn't happen and, just to note, never will. I moved to Italy because I fell in love with Brigid Borgo.

Brigid Borgo stands elegantly on the shore of Lake Trasimeno. She had been derelict for about twenty years before I found her and made her mine. After so many years of neglect, there was a lot of work still to do to refurn her to her 1920s glory.

Sophia moved in soon after I got enough renovations finished to make the house habitable. Sophia now lives on the first floor while I enjoy the views from the second floor, and we share the communal areas on the ground floor.

The cantina was once a cellar for the wine, made from the vines surrounding the property. There is no wine there now, just some cobwebby wine-making paraphernalia and empty barrels sitting in the corner which I'm afraid to move in case of snakes and scorpions. I found some bottles of homemade wine there when I first moved in. Sophia and I did attempt to test some, but it was not a wine that was made to rest and become vintage. Instead of saying it was a cheeky little red with tones of cherry and oak, we concluded it was a mouldy little red with flavours of insect and must.

I will get around to moving the barrels outside someday, but for now they can sit gathering dust in the corner. We have enough room in the rest of the cantina for what we use it for– storing our wedding equipment. Arches, rolls of fabric, strings of lights, urns, pedestals, statues, picture frames, chair covers, sashes, and lots of signs of love.

I mean that literally. We have 17 different styles of signs with 'Love' written on them.

After my call with Paolo, I found Sophia in the cantina. "Bad news... Sarah Murphy just called, and she's pregnant with twins."

"And this is bad because?" asked Sophia, peeling off a lump of candle wax from the glass pane of one of the 40 lanterns to be cleaned after our last wedding.

"Because it's another postponement to next year... I'm supposed to be retiring next year and at this rate of impregnation I will have a full year of postponed weddings."

"Don't worry, by next summer I should have my wedding wings and be able to run them solo," Sophia said confidently. Perhaps she could. She had been a great apprentice and would soon have enough confidence to run weddings solo. However, with the postponements I would still need to be involved as the couples were contracted to me.

Sophia was in one of my "So You Want To Be A Wedding Planner?" conference talks three years ago. We hit it off. I could see she really had what it took to be an excellent wedding planner, and I was in need of an assistant. Within weeks she had moved from the south of Italy into Brigid Borgo and had not only become invaluable to me as a wedding assistant but also as a personal assistant. She was all the things I was not, a talented designer and patient with the most troublesome guests. I, on the other hand, liked to stay behind the scenes, do all the logical stuff–timetables, transport organising, table plans, vendor co-ordination–rather than the fluffy stuff.

"It also means gaps in the season, and you know I don't like gaps in the season, it ruins my rhythm."

"You mean it stops you being a robot? Working 16-hour days, for 20 weeks in a row is not healthy. A break will be good for you." She was referring to the fact that from mid-April to mid-October every year I had at least one weddings per week, sometimes three or four.

"No, a break means I'll get sick. My adrenalin drops and–"

"And you have time to notice your body is crying out for a break. It's unnatural to keep going at that pace," she said, lecturing me like a mother scorning her teenager for partying too much, even though she was nearly 25 years my junior.

"That is why I am retiring."

"That is why you should be happy about having three weeks off dotted through the season."

"Two weeks off..." I corrected her. "I got a late booking to fill the cancelled September wedding."

"Yes well, two weeks off. One of those weeks is next week so plan something relaxing." Sophia could be a bossy-boots when she wanted to be, I was discovering. Another trait a wedding planner needed; to take leadership and give staff and wedding vendors clear instruction of what needs to be done on the day of a wedding in a friendly, team-building way.

I pulled over a chair and started to work through the lantern pile with Sophia. Both she and Paolo had made a good point. I should take advantage of the free time and do something relaxing. I was getting too old for this burning the candle at both ends malarky. And there was nothing I loved more than taking time out to spend time with my newfound love of gardening.

"You are right, the orto could badly do with some attention. The tomato plants need propping up and the lettuce needs thinning out. That's what I'll do next week, work on the vegetable garden."

With that, my phone buzzed. "Hello, you again," I said in a cheery voice.

"It's Paolo," I mouthed at Sophia. I didn't need to emphasise my words so much with her, but it was like a private joke to do now and again, as she was an expert lip reader since being nearly completely deaf as a child. Her hearing was still not 100 per cent but her lip-reading ability in several languages was spectacular. At this point in our friendship she could nearly skip the lip-reading and just know what I was thinking. But when Paolo called, she didn't need to do either. My body language said it all.

"I have you on speaker phone as I'm cleaning lanterns with Sophia, so don't say anything too raunchy."

"Oh, you ruined the reason why I called now." His smooth, deep voice during the many long calls since we got together again in Rome always made me a little light-headed.

"I'm just thinking, did you say you had next week off, because of the bride who is a bit pregnant?" he asked.

"Yes, I'm just talking with Sophia about how I am going to relax working on my vegetable garden."

"While that sounds fun, but how about spending the week with me in Florence instead of with your cucumbers?" Sophia snorted laughing at what Paolo just said. Practically every fruit and vegetable in Italy has a sexual innuendo attached to it, so I avoid mentioning vegetable names in any conversation.

"Yes, she will go with you Paolo," shouted Sophia across the room. "Take her away, please. She needs to relax and have some romance in her life. I'll stay here and keep her cucumbers happy."

Now they were both laughing at their inside Italian joke.

Before I could get a word in edgeways between both of them shouting arrangements about my week off at each other, Paolo wound up the conversation with, "Okay, then I'll pick you up on Friday. You are coming with me to Florence. Have her ready to go Sophia."

2

Why do men think women are better at carrying cakes? 'Tanto 80th Auguri Zia Ciara' was neatly iced on the boxed cake I was left carrying from the carpark.

An 80th birthday party was not quite how I expected to spend the first day of my rare summer week off. Paolo had 'forgotten' to mention it, like he had forgotten to mention we would be staying in his aunt's apartment.

So instead of running around making a young couple's dream wedding day in Italy happen that weekend, I was in my favourite city in Italy, spending the week with my 'friend' Paolo's aged aunt. I had already decided that was not going to last long. I would stay a night, perhaps two at the most, and then make my excuses and go back to my beloved Trasimeno. This was not my idea of a romantic week away with Paolo, having not seen him for over a month.

After parking Mabel Carr, my red Morgan Convertible, in a private underground car park out of the full sun, we walked along the Arno towards the Ponte Vecchio and turned down a side street off the fashionable cobbled street of Tournabouni.

"Here we are," said Paolo, gripping the large bouquet he had carefully chosen for his aunt. We stood on a narrow, cobbled road facing magnificent double doors with geometric shapes carved into the weathered wood. The doors were impressive, but so were the five similar doors we just passed on the same street.

There were no other openings in the wall apart from a foot high grey stone framed window with its own tiny wooden doors. Is that where the elves get in?" I asked Paolo.

"No, it is a wine window." He laughed. "They are particular to Tuscany. They were created during the Plague and Renaissance, so that wine merchants could sell wine from their homes and cellars without the need for physical contact. They were popular as the wine was cheaper than from taverns as they did not to have to pay staff. Wine was probably a very good trade to be in at that time as everyone was encouraged to drink at least a litre of wine a day to stay healthy in those days."

"Gosh!" My romantic image of the Renaissance in Florence rapidly flipped from one of elegant ladies and gentlemen linked arm in arm walking around in grand dress wear, to ladies and gentlemen linked arm in arm to stop each other from falling over drunk.

Large black iron handles hanging from the nostrils of gargoyle heads distinguished the door we stood at from the others. A brass plate with five bell buttons invited you to choose who you wanted to visit.

To the first-time visitor, the solid wooden double doors on the street might appear as just fancy garage doors. But they were anything but that. Beyond many of these ancient street doors in Italian towns, there is a whole matrix into an elegant world on the other side.

I stepped in closer to the door to avoid being run over by a Fiat 500 whizzing down the pathless street, followed by a moped scooter powered by a guy who obviously thought himself as the next Evel Knievel.

'Sig. C. Bocelli' was the brass bell Paolo chose. The second option under it caught my eye: Artista Raphael Corbo.

"Is Artista a first name in Italy?" I asked Paolo curiously.

"No, it's just someone full of his own importance." He smirked as the door buzzed to be pushed open. Paolo was familiar with where he was going. He had added to the worn shininess of the stone entrance with his many years visiting his aunt. Beyond the door did not fail to impress. A short, arched entrance opened into a paved courtyard of dappled light. Birds flitted amongst the small grove of trees in the enclosed garden beyond. Wide marble staircases sat on both sides of the surrounding portico, inviting you up to the continuous balcony that led to three front doors on either side.

The sound of the central water fountain added to the instant tranquility, complemented by the classical music drifting down. The sound increased as Paolo led me up the stairs to the door at the far end of the balcony on the righthand side.

I don't have old relatives to visit, I never have. My expectations of what I imagined an octogenarian's birthday party to be like were stereo-typical; A little old lady fixing her knitting, sitting in a corner of the dusty apartment with a few people fussing around her. What I was greeted with was quite different.

The teak door swung open and there stood a woman a little taller than me, dressed in a crisp white pantsuit, the perfect background to the long Mariner Anchor link-gold Gucci necklace draped around her neck. A broad smile fixed on her elegant face.

"Paolo, my dear boy," she exuded with genuine Italian affection. "It is so good to see you again, it has been too long."

"It has only been a month, Aunt Ciara."

"But that is too long. You need to come more often. I miss your little face." She talked to him as if he was still eight.

"Aunt, this is my friend Daisy, she's Irish, so I think you will like her."

"Fantastic that a woman has finally pinned Paolo down, and a good Irish woman at that."

"It's not like that, Aunt." Paolo hastened to add.

"Nonsense, look at her, she's beautiful, get a ring on her finger soon before she is whipped up." Before I could say anything, Paolo retrieved the cake from my hands and put on a side table so that Zia Ciara could embrace me and marry me off to her nephew. Paolo twitched his shoulders uneasily, trying to find his way out of the hole of embarrassment his aunt was digging for him. I raised my eyebrows at him to ease his discomfort as my face was pressed against her white hair ingeniously pinned atop of her head in a perfect chignon. Her blue eyes were still as clear as those of a young woman. Age had not affected her.

"Nonsense, life is too short to wait until the perfect moment." She put her arm lightly on my waist and led me down the hallway, followed by Paolo. "My first husband was Irish, a wonderful man. I love Ireland. I spent many wonderful times there sampling the whiskey. He died young, tragically, but life goes on."

We entered a bright, fresco-ceilinged living room where about 20 people filled the room comfortably with chinking glasses and prosecco flowing. A string quartet was playing in the corner. The crowd looked like they were more likely to be discussing the next opera they were going to see or yacht they were going to buy rather than knitting patterns or commodes.

"Let me show you to your room first so you know where you are staying and where you can escape to if my friends get too boring," she laughed. I liked her. "They're mostly from the art world. If you are interested in art, you'll find them fascinating, but if not, they will be as dull as dishwater to you," she said, leading me down the hall, followed by Paolo carrying our bags.

"I do like art. I have no real knowledge of it, but I like art galleries and dabbling in acrylics now and then. You have some nice pieces," I said admiring the eclectic mix of art lining the walls of the hallway leading from the party room.

"That's a bathroom down the hall, but you also have an ensuite from your room here," she said, unlocking a double door into a frescoed room with a four-poster bed draped in burgundy velvet. "Keep the door locked when you are not in here today," she said lowly. "I have some very nosy neighbours and I like to keep them in the dark about what is in the bedrooms. I think Raphael thinks I have a precious work of art hanging in this room, and he would be sorely disappointed if he saw it was just a terrible painting of me as a child. But I like to keep him guessing. His constant angles to get in here amuse me greatly." She opened the door and handed me the key. "This is the ensuite. Annette, my cleaning lady, left towels in there, but if you need extra, just ask."

Ciara noticed I had stopped to stare at the painting. I couldn't help but stop. "That's the painting. I call it The Ugly Child." A podgy child with double chins and a stubborn, if not darn right evil, look on her face stared back at me. It wasn't just ugly, but badly proportioned.

"I was about six when my mother got me to pose for it. I was going to throw it out several times, but I have decided to leave that task to Paolo after I die. I won't be offended, Paolo, when you do it!" If she was podgy as a kid, there were no signs of it now with her great jaw line flanked with beautiful lines of wisdom.

"How lovely to have a painting by your mother. So she was a portrait artist?" I loved finding out the history of people's families through objects.

"No, mostly landscapes, but she was good at portraits, too. She had a job as a life model for an artist called George Ballini and then she became his apprentice, to learn to do portraits. It's unfortunate that she never painted my father's portrait. I have some photos of my mother but there was only one photo of him. It has long since been lost... He was killed in the war the Christmas before she painted the Ugly Child. She was pregnant at the time. My father never got to meet my sister–Paolo's mother."

Her voice drifted a little before coming back stronger. "This wasn't one of her best pieces, but it's a painting of me, supposedly, and painted by my mother and that's why I keep it... And it's covering up a hole in the wall," she confided with a smirk before turning to Paolo, who had made a quick trip to the loo. "I need to get back to my other guests. Now settle in and, in your own time, come join the party for drinks before we go to the restaurant." She closed the door gently behind her.

"It is an ugly painting, isn't it?" Paolo said, joining me as I gazed at the framed canvas. "My grandmother was supposedly good at painting, but other than being ugly, there's something off about this painting and I can't quite put my finger on what it is. Aunt Ciara was a good-looking child. I've seen some photos. I can't understand why her mother painted her looking so... unattractive."

I could see a likeness of Paolo across the mouth in the painting. But even my amateur art brain could spot something was wrong. My eye for detail always catches the minor things. I would be a great continuity person in a movie.

"It's the eyes. There are too many reflections of light in the pupils," I said, referring to the three tiny white dots. "There should only be one."

"You know you could be right. The eyes are good, but they don't look right and it's just... ugly. I think it was rushed. I think she was pregnant with my mother when she painted it. Maybe her hormones affected her or something."

"That's what your aunt Ciara said, she was pregnant at the time. It's sad that your mother never knew her father. Did you ever see the picture of him?"

"Yes, I have it. Why?"

"Your aunt thinks it's missing. She hasn't seen it for years. Perhaps you should give it to her."

"I'll bring it with me the next time. Anyway, shall we get back to the party? I'm starving."

Even though I had only been in the room for five minutes, I had already mislaid my handbag. Just as I walked past the door to check in the far corner where we had left our suitcases, the handle was pushed down and a guy with small spectacles and a moustache and goatee stepped in before seeing Paolo and jumping back in alarm. "I'm sorry I thought this was the bathroom."

"Just down the hall," Paolo smiled confidently.

"Thank you." He backed out of the room coyly. As I was behind the door, he hadn't seen me, but I had enough of a glance of him to sum him up.

"I'll bet you a cocktail that he's the nosy neighbour your aunt was talking about," I commented to Paolo as I grabbed my bag. It had somehow found its way under the bed.

"I bet you two cocktails that he's a painter," Paolo responded.

"Hmm, interesting bet. What makes you think that?"

"He has one of those beards and moustaches that painters have in movies."

"And your argument is that artists can only paint when they have those moustaches and beards, is that it?" I put my arms around his neck and kissed his lips. "I'll happily take the bet if that is all you are going on, but I think you will be owing me three mojitos."

"Well, let's go ask him if he is an artist or a nosy neighbour."

"Don't you dare!"

"Come on," he said, opening the door and waving me out. "I'm going to ask him."

3

Outside in the lounge, some more guests had arrived. To a point that the room was nearly crowded. No one seemed to be taking any notice of the heated discussion between the two women in the hallway. They were both in their late twenties with opposite looks, one had long dark hair in a ponytail and a voluptuous figure while the other was a tall thin blonde. Both had fingers pointing at each other and speaking rapidly in an eastern European language I didn't recognise, until the end when the black-haired girl stormed out the front door and then blond called after her in English, "Julia, wait!". Not being able to see the nosy artistic guy was a relief, as I am sure Paolo would have said something.

Aunt Ciara was standing with her back to us, on the other side of the room leaning on the grand piano talking to a woman with a drink in hand, sitting on the piano stool for comfort rather than to play. An elegantly dressed, grey-haired man had his arm around her waist. I was a little taken aback when I saw him give Aunt Ciara's butt a squeeze. My infantilising instinctive response was to go over and slap his hand like they were two children 30 years my junior rather than two grown adults 30 years my senior. I followed Paolo's lead over to where she was.

"There you are Paolo. This is my friend Signore Valentino Bruni; he is a restoration master down at the Uffizi," said his aunt, not noticing I was three steps behind.

"Ah Paolo, so good to meet you at last. Your wonderful aunt has been telling me so much about you. Although I think we met about two years ago at Christmas party here, just in passing, before your aunt would accept to go on a date with me," the man said.

I circled around the other side of the piano and glanced back. Paolo was being his charming self, but I could see by his eye movement he was judging the white-bearded elder speaking to him. While I would genuinely find this man interesting, I felt this was a family moment and I couldn't help but put my planner hat on and start gathering a few stray glasses from the polished furniture while Paolo bonded with his aunt's man friend.

"Waitress... go get my girlfriend a glass of champagne, the service is very 'slack'." It was one of those moments where you know the demand is directed at you, but I was the one feeling embarrassed at the person mistaking me for a staff member rather than a guest.

"I am sorry," I said, turning around and placing the voice with the bespectacled guy that had walked into our room.

I had a better view of him now. He was tall and in his late 50s, a little older than Paolo. He had a presence but in a wrong way. What I mean is, he could have been a strikingly handsome man if he wasn't dressed like a caricature of a suffering artist; sporting a handlebar moustache and a goatee, thick dyed black hair, and a silk scarf tied around his neck.

Paolo might win the bet after all, although what he was wearing didn't fit the artiste persona; double denim, black jeans, and a dark denim shirt.

Linked tightly to his arm was an equally tall, slender blonde woman in her late 20s. She would be termed as good looking, but an expression of being completely fed up, bored and not having her way ruined her beauty. It was not just from this situation, but permanently from being a spoilt child, I guessed. I had heard him introduce her to another guest earlier. "This is my girlfriend, Anna, from the Czech Republic. She's a model here in Florence."

I always apologise, even when I am not at fault. "I'm sorry, I am not working here, I'm a guest, but let me find a waiter for you."

"Oh," his eyes dropped up and down judgingly. "You're a friend of Ciara's? Are you in the Commission?"

"The Commission? What's that?"

"You obviously don't know Ciara that well then. I'm talking about the Commission for Looted Art in Europe... most of the people here are in it or connected to it in some way. Ciara and Valentino would probably be the most prominent activists. I would be more active, but I am far too busy with my art. I am an artist and a dedicated one at that. A lot of these here claim to be artists but never seem to produce anything."

Crap. I owed Paolo two cocktails. I guessed he was Artista Raphael, the name we saw on the bell label. "I'm looking forward to spending the weekend here, it's a wonderful apartment, isn't it?"

"Yes, they all are... I live in this building too." My mind gave me brownie points for my accurate amateur sleuth guessing. "Mine is on the opposite side. I'm not sure which view I prefer, Ciara's or mine. Both our families have been in these buildings for generations. Well, mine more so than hers, she is here by... default."

He could see confusion slapped on my face. But I was not confused about the "default" statement, more so of why he felt the need to tell a complete stranger.

"This apartment was the Ballini's family property and George Ballini left it to Ciara's mother and Ciara, even though neither of them were related to him. It was solely held by Marquese families like mine up to their arrival... Shame... Ciara is lovely and she was here nearly 20 years before I was even born, but I can't help but feel a little regret that it is still not solely held by nobility."

What a snob.

"Is your apartment the same as this?" I asked, popping a stuffed olive into my mouth.

"Yes, but as I said, I think I have a better view of the Arno."

Ha, I had received the information needed. Now Paolo owed me the cocktails. If this guy's apartment was the same layout, he knew where the bathroom was and had come into our room just to have a snoop. He was the nosy neighbour.

"So, what do you paint?" I said, trying to change the subject, before his toffy,   I-am-greater-than-thou-you-are-not-worthy-to-be-in-my-presence attitude made my stomach tighten any further.

"I specialise in beauty wherever I find it." His girlfriend's nostrils flared and I couldn't help but notice she needed a lipstick top up as she bit the inside of her cheek.

"Is there somewhere I can see your work?" Again, I was trying to make the mood less intense when really it was not my responsibility to do so.

"He's just like the others. He finishes nothing," the blonde girlfriend said, rolling her eyes.

"I work tirelessly. Great art takes time." He spat the words out through his suddenly tightened lips. She had hit a sensitive spot.

"Yes, and great weddings cost money," she snapped back, unhooking her arm from his, "I am going to get a drink." As she did so, I glimpsed a thin gold ring on her ring finger with a small diamond. I guessed it was supposed to be a temporary one, just for the proposal, but it was now dulled and it seemed her finger was waiting quite some time for its 'real' engagement ring replacement. So, he was old money; had assets but was cash poor.

I was trying to suppress my need to fill the silence that was left by Anna's exit from our company. It's a personality fault I am still working on. The instant perspiration and awkwardness overcomes me and I usually sacrifice my cool demeaner by asking a stupid question.

"Do you find painting difficult?"

Raphael stared at me as if reading my soul and searching my face, wondering where such a stupid question came from.

"That is something that no one has asked me before... but it is an excellent question. Painting is very difficult. People think it comes naturally to those who are gifted, but we artists struggle. We fight with the paint to achieve perfection. For me the difficulty is getting the purity of the face, I have no problem with still lifes, I am as good as the masters, some of which I feel were over-rated, and a conversation for another time... but the face is difficult."

I prayed there would not be another time for that conversation, or any other conversation with him, for that matter.

He gazed past my head as if imagining the strokes he would try when he returned to his current work in progress but then snapped back, "You mentioned you are staying here, with Ciara... how is your room?"

Was he coming on to me?

"It's very comfortable, Paolo... my friend... has stayed here with his aunt a lot."

"Ah Paolo, yes, I remember him. what does he do again?"

"He's in hotel management."

"Hmm..." he snorted, sipping the drink he had taken from a passing tray. It looked like he was using it as a periscope as he held it to his mouth and scanned around the room again. "Ciara has some nice pieces of art. I am sure the bedrooms must have some nice pieces too. I'd love to see them."

Of course he wasn't flirting, he was just interested in seeing what paintings Ciara was harbouring. A rapid knock on the front door was my saving grace from another awkward pause in the conversation. "I'll get it," I said nearly too enthusiastically at the welcomed opportunity to break away from the 'artista'.

"That must be the surprise I ordered for Ciara," said Valentino, a step behind me. I took advantage of my younger years to get to the door before him, but I was more surprised than he was to see who was at the door.

4

"Oh my God, Daisy!" Davide screeched, throwing his lanky body around me. "How amazing to see you! What are you doing here?" he said, hugging me with caution, as not to crush the large white tea rose in the lapel of his dark pink suit.

"Signora Bocelli is Paolo's aunt, and he brought me along to her party. What are you doing here? I don't think I have ever seen you outside a wedding environment." Davide was my favourite florist and although he was based in Tuscany, he was sought after for weddings all over Italy.

"Wait, Paolo is here too? This is too much! Let's hope it's not a rerun of Rome!" Davide had the habit of always saying the worst things at the wrong moment.

"Are you delivering flowers or here for the party?" I asked, trying to brush on to the next conversation before Valentino could ask what happened in Rome. It was not something I wanted to get into.

"Work, unfortunately, no party for this bad boy today. But this has been my favourite commission, Evvv-errr," he said with full, close eye contact, resting his hand on my arm as if confiding his most secret of secrets.

"There you are!" he said, quickly changing attention to Valentino, as they gave each other the two cheek air welcome everyone gives in Italy. And then he threw open his arms to Paolo who had come to the hallway, with an equal amount of enthusiasm he gave to me, which made me feel less special.

"Paolo, could you ensure your aunt or none of the guests come into the hallway I want this to be a surprise," Valentino asked excitedly and Paolo graciously followed orders.

"It took a tonne of time, but oh my God it is so wonderful. I hope you are pleased with it," oozed Davide to Valentino, easing open the front door and ushering in his two assistants carrying flowers in a porcelain vase that had a painting on it of two cherubs, one kissing the other.

It was a shabby flower arrangement, but in perfect dishevelment. Half open tulips, poppy seed heads, geraniums, irises, full roses. "Is that a real butterfly?" I asked, pointing at the butterfly sitting delicately on one iris. "It is real, but dead," said Davide. "I didn't kill it, I bought it from a lepidopterist."

"It's a masterpiece," gasped Valentino. "Here, set it up here on this plinth."

Davide worked on angling it perfectly central to the archway into the room. At the base of the vase, he arranged a small nest with three blue eggs and two plums.

"This has been a wonderful commission to do Valentino, and such a thoughtful idea. Thank you so much for asking me to do it. The guests are going to go wild." Davide was right. The guests did go wild when the doors opened to the hallway.

As the oooohs and aaahhs filled the room, I stood to the side with Davide.

"Davide, the flowers are beautiful, but I seem to be missing the meaning behind this. Why is everybody so ecstatic? I mean, I know your work is good and all but... I asked.

"Oh honey, you don't know about the Vase of Flowers?" Davide said sympathetically, making me feel like I had just failed a basic reading test. "Well... neither did I until Valentino commissioned me to do this and told me the whole story." He said, comforting my stupidity. "My flower sculpture–as I like to call it–is the exact replica of a still life painting by Jan van Huysum, which was stolen from Italy by the Nazis in the 1940s. When it was being shipped across the border from Italy to Germany, a German corporal took it from the stolen hoard and sent it to his wife in Germany.

"The painting was missing for decades. Then, a few weeks after the fall of the Berlin Wall, a German family started trying to sell the picture to the Italian State and they have even threatened to destroy it unless a ransom is paid. Signora Ciara and Valentino have campaigned tirelessly to get it back to Italy, to its rightful place in the Uffizi Gallery," said Davide in a hushed tone, as if he was all knowl-edgeable on all things art and giving me a guided tour.

"Okay, you can come in now," called out Valentino, who seemed more apprehensive than what was normal when presenting a bunch of flowers to his girlfriend.

"Oh my goodness, Valentino. What have you done?" Ciara's eyes instantly filled with tears, her hands clasped to her mouth in disbe-lief. "It's amazing. What a wonderful surprise."

"This isn't the surprise... this is," started Valentino, holding the side table and easing himself awkwardly down to one knee.

"Darling Ciara, I could not fulfil your dream of being able to get the painting back to Italy. Perhaps this is a little compensation until that day comes. In the meantime, Ciara I'd like to ask you to fulfil a dream of mine... Ciara darling, will you marry me?" The room suddenly fell silent after a group communal gasp. Now I understood his apprehension.

The antique grandfather clock in the hallway ticked louder than I had previously noticed. A look of horror crossed Paolo's face.

"I would be delighted," beamed Ciara, as she took his hands in hers and a bystander helped Valentino back up to his feet, before he kissed his new fiancé on her waiting lips. The room applauded, the band started to play, 'Congratulations'.

Paolo looked paler than before, gulping down the glass of prosecco he was holding as he crossed the room to my side. "What are they thinking of? Getting married at their age?" he hissed in my ear.

"Love knows no bounds," I joked, feeding into his horror and loving his loathing. "Your aunt looks delighted Paolo, you should be happy for her." A waiter refilled his glass.

"But it's odd at their age, isn't it?" He knocked back the prosecco like it was a shot. "Do you think he is after her money? She's very well off."

"Are you just thinking of your inheritance?" My forehead wrinkled in amusement at his concern.

"No, it's just odd... at their age."

"I think getting married at any age is odd." My disclosure is nothing new to Paolo, we've had this conversation before of my intention never to get married.

"Oh yes, I forgot that you're so set against getting married," he grumbled, lifting his glass to his lips and then looking at the glass as if it had played an evil trick on him for being empty again.

Davide threw his arms around Ciara before anyone else could get to her. "Congratulations!"

"Em, thank you... are you a friend of Daisy's?" Ciara said, easing from the grip of the pink clad stranger.

"Oh well yes, more work colleagues really. She's a great wedding planner you know? She'll be able to organise your wedding for you in no time at all."

"I didn't know that!" gleamed Ciara. "Indeed, it would be great if you could plan the wedding Daisy. The sooner the better, at our age we can't afford to do long engagements."

"Good point," laughed Valentino. His mouth was full of laughter, but not the kind of laughter that filled a room. It was the laughter of the heart, a kind of soft, hooting laugh, that flutters into the room like a handful of rose petal confetti. "How fast can we get married, Daisy?"

"Well, usually you need to give three months' notice but perhaps we can get a special dispensation if you really want to rush it," I said feebly. I really didn't want to have to plan a quick wedding, especially in the middle of my busy wedding season.

Paolo wasn't laughing. He seemed to be the only one not finding the whole prospect of a quick wedding romantic and exciting. "I didn't realise this was also going to be an engagement party... Are you sure about this, Aunt?" Paolo was being snarky.

"Third time lucky and all that jazz." Ciara was not rising to the bait of her nephew's disapproval.

"Davide, why don't you join us for dinner? We can fit an extra place, can't we, Ciara?" said Valentino, putting his hand on Davide's shoulder and leading him over to a tray of drinks.

"Of course! You must join us," agreed Ciara. "There's a place free at the table as Filippo won't be able to make it. He had a class or an emergency at the studio or something. So you can take Filippo's place."

"I can never refuse a party invite," gleamed Davide, clasping Ciara's hand as if she was his precious long-lost grandmother.

"Okay everybody," she shouted out to the room. "Gather your belongings and let's go to the restaurant, they are waiting for us."

Glasses clinked and conversations became more muffled as the hungry gang shuffled out the front door.

"It's just a short walk," Ciara linking my arm walking down the steps from her apartment. "I overheard my neighbour Raphael boasting about his apartment being better than mine," she said smugly in a hushed voiced.

"He was saying he had a better view of the Arno."

"It probably would be better if he ever opened his curtains. In all the years he has lived there by himself, he has kept the curtains tightly shut and never switches on a light. I've seen no one go in there, not even Anna, his girlfriend. He's a bit of strange chap, but I find his strangeness amusing. But don't worry, there are plenty of other interesting people at this party."

"Did I hear you speak of me, Aunt?" Paolo caught up with us and linked her other arm.

"No, I don't think so."

"You mentioned interesting people? I thought you were trying to sell me off to Daisy again."

"Don't fool yourself Paolo, there are some much more interesting people here," she joked back. "Daisy, I have put you sitting next to Natasha, she's a Russian Art Historian. I think you will find her fascinating." The smile on my face immediately hopped from my lips onto Paolo's face. He knew how much I hated sitting beside random people at dinner, especially anyone intense.

"Wonderful," I said, trying to sound enthusiastic, but I was anything but.

5

Carefully placed name cards on the table made it impossible to get away from who we were assigned to suffer the next two or three hours with. Aunt Clara had the rightful place at the top of the table, Paolo had been placed on her right, and Valentino on her left. Like she was the quiz master, and they were the opposing competitors. The three of them immediately went into a deep huddle of conversation led by Valentino.

My place was between Paolo and this Russian woman. Opposite me was Anna, the model and the nosy neighbour Raphael. Davide had already struck up conversation with the biker looking chap opposite him down the table. The rest of the table seemed to all know each other and had split off into their own chat space. If we had to make a comparison, our end of the table was definitely the more fun end to be on, and that said a lot.

I decided to make the most of it. Perhaps this could be interesting if the woman beside me and Anna relaxed a little and stopped looking like they were guarding the crown jewels.

"Hi, I'm Daisy, a friend of Paolo's, Ciara's nephew," I said just as I sat, offering my hand. The Russian women was not that much older than me but still made me feel small by examining me over the top brim of her red-winged spectacles. Her black shiny bobbed hair with perfect bangs looked like it had just been cut and set on top of her head and ordered not to move. It fell perfectly about her pale face.

"I'm Doctor Natasha Verbotski."

"From your accent, I take it you are not Italian?" I joked, trying to get the poker out of her ass. It didn't work.

"I'm an art historian and curator of 20th-century art at the State Russian Museum in St Petersburg and a consultant to Sotheby's–the English auction house, in London. Ciara and Valentino are my respected friends so I would not miss the opportunity of her birthday celebration."

"How interesting." This was going to be a bag of laughs. "It's my first time meeting Ciara and Valentino. Will you be visiting the Uffizi while here then?"

"Of course. It is like my Italian home. I work with them a lot. That is how I know Valentino and have got to know Ciara. Valentino is a fabulous art restorer, he's very much respected throughout the art world," she said, directing her words across the table to pull Valentino into the conversation.

"Thank you for your kind words Natasha." Valentino nodded, raising his water glass to her. I liked him. He had kind, smiling eyes. His elbows were on the table, his wrinkled wise hands rubbing together slightly as the waiter filled his wineglass. "I used to restore art," he said, explaining himself to me. "But my hands have become a little too shaky, so I am now more of a... teacher, but it is difficult to get apprentices these days, everyone wants to be the best instantly, they are not willing to put in the years like we did. Ten, twenty, thirty years, in my case a lifetime, to reach a level of semi-mastery.

"You make yourself sound like Filippo. You are much more than just a teacher." Tutted Natasha. "You illustrate how to do mastery Filippo teaches tourists how to copy Rembrandt."

"You are being unjust to poor Filippo," said Valentino, trying to hold back his smile. "Although one of us should drop by the studio on the way home to ensure he has left no lit cigarettes burning in an ashtray, he can be quite forgetful. We don't want the Uffizi burning down."

"Stop being such a scorned lover Natasha, Filippo's work is flawless." Raphael dipped his bread into the mix of olive oil and balsamic vinegar he had poured on his side plate. His eyes held Natasha's as he basked in the loss of speech his words had caused her.

My constant need to fix things kicked in again. "So are you a member of the Looted Art Commission too?" I asked, passing her the basket of bread. I think she appreciated I was throwing her a life buoy. Her shoulders relaxed a bit.

"Yes, I think most of us here are. I am actually the chief director of it."

"Oh. What does the commission do exactly? Davide was telling me earlier that the Nazis stole some paintings during the War and-"

"SOME?!" she practically screeched at the shock of my stupidity.

"The Nazis looted over 6,000 pieces of art and cultural property. Since the commission was formed, we have been instrumental in the restitution of over 3,500 objects, such as paintings, books and silver, to their rightful owners. But our work is far from over." She paused to take a mouthful of the starter of poached egg with black truffle and potato cream that had been placed in front of all the seated guests.

I needed to think of something intelligent to say to redeem myself. Something that would get her to talk about her passion. "If you don't mind me asking, with so many works of art missing for so long, when one is found, how do you know whether or not it's a forgery?"

"It is a good question," she put down her fork and I felt relieved. "The number of avant-garde fakes out there today is unbelievable, probably more than the number of genuine works. Forgers can perfectly reproduce the paints, pigments, binders and canvas. They thought they had all the corners covered until a friend of mine found a magic ingredient." Doctor Natasha smirked, taking another mouthful while watching Raphael flush and twitch with agitation.

"What was the magic ingredient?" I was no longer trying to fill in silences I was genuinely interested.

"It is thanks to the atomic bomb. Atomic bombs basically blew up a lot of the forgery art world." She rested her fork back down on her finished plate.

"I don't understand. What has the atomic bomb to do with art forgery?" I asked while topping up her glass and mine with a soft pink, fruity Santa Cristina Rosé.

"An art friend of mine in Russia, together with a scientist, found two artificial isotopes that iron clad identifying forgeries in these paintings." She said matter-of-factly, as if that explained everything.

Valentino came to my rescue explaining further. "The world's nuclear nations exploded 550 nuclear weapons during tests between the years of 1945 and 1963. All above-ground detonations were then banned. One of the unintended side effects of these tests was the release of two artificial isotopes that only form during a nuclear bomb blast. These isotopes were absorbed by the soil and incorporated into the cellular structure of plants. In fact, they were absorbed by just about everything–soil, plants, animals, people–everybody alive in between 1945 and 1963 have elevated levels of these isotopes compared to everything that lived before that time."

"I still don't understand, how this affects forgers? Does it make their heads spin?" The rosé and prosecco mix on an empty stomach was loosening my humour.

"Well, not quite," chuckled Valentino. "When, say, a flax plant growing in contaminated soil is processed into linseed oil, which is a common pigment binding agent used by artists, those isotopes remain. This now provides art scientists with an easily identifiable timestamp--if these isotopes are present, the work of art clearly cannot have been done before 1945."

Now I was getting it. "Oh okay, so flax in the fields absorbs these two isotopes from previous nuclear fallout, and the flax is used to make linseed oil, which is then used in paint production, and so the isotopes are present in the forgeries?" I summarised to confirm to myself what he was saying.

"Yes, you've got it," smiled Natasha. The blush wine was softening her mood too.

"I'm sure that put a lot of forgers out of business." I finished my first pasta course and resisted the urge to lick the plate.

"Yes, it did. For instance, some years ago, Raphael thought he had found the painting of The Vase of Flowers. Then the original reappeared and thanks to the Basner test method–that is what it is called– we could tell the forgery was not the original... isn't that right Raphael?" Natasha was getting her own back on his earlier snide remark at her love life.

"You found a forgery, Raphael?" piped up Davide, who had been in raucous conversation with the guy sitting on the other side of Natasha. "Where on earth did you find it?"

"In France, at a car boot sale. I thought, or should I say knew, it was just an imitation when I bought it, but then Ciara and Valentino saw it and thought it was the real thing. It did not fool me." He put his arm across the back of Anna's chair and I knew he was man-spreading under the table.

"You were fooled as much as they were," jousted Natasha "I remember. You thought you were going to make a fortune and lapped up being interviewed by the newspapers." I felt like I was watching an episode of Scooby Doo, with Raphael's big break as the hero of the art world, being foiled by a meddling Russian woman.

"So, the atomic bomb saved the art world," slipped in Paolo. I didn't think he had been listening as he had been in deep conversation with his aunt, probably about his soon-to-be step uncle.

Anna had not spoken nor eaten much of the first or second course that most of us had polished off at this stage. I felt like asking her for her portion of pasta with Sicilian pesto. It was so delicious, but I went for something more conversational.

"So, Anna, how do you enjoy living in Italy, do you miss your friends back in the Czech Republic?"

Raphael answered before she could say anything. "Not at all. Her friend Julia came with her when she moved here six years ago."

"That bitch, is not my friend anymore, she is more your friend."

"Oh, come on Anna, don't be jealous now." Raphael patted her condescendingly on the back.

"You spend more time with her than me."

I could feel my neck redden, I really am not good when couples have a tiff around me, I never know where to look and being stuck at a dinner table facing them, it limited me to staring at Anna's bosom or at the ceiling above her head. I chose the ceiling.

"That is because we are working together. She is posing for me." He petted her cheek with his index finger as if she was a cat with some cobwebs stuck in her whiskers.

"I pose for you," Anna pouted.

"Yes, but she is different, not as beautiful of course, but she has a very different look to you, which is helping me finish a particular work. You know that." He leaned over and she accepted his kiss.

"Ralphy, I am not feeling well, can we go soon?" She was still pouting.

"Of course. As soon as we finish dinner, we will go honey, okay?" He was dripping in sweetly sickness.

Her bottom lip protruded as she nibbled some of her food.

"Hey Daisy, I heard you say you are a wedding planner." Raphael lifted his chin in my direction as if that extra inch higher would make the words reach me stronger.

I nodded, slowly taking a sip of my wine, knowing what was coming next and dreading hearing it. Three, two, one and...

"Next year we will marry. Maybe you can organise it for us Daisy?"

Every event I turn up at develops into someone discussing their wedding and expecting me to plan it. I glanced at her ring again. Her elegant fingers was crying out for more expensive decoration, but it was not just her ring that looked out of place, her stubby nails were traced with encrusted clay. I would expect someone like her to have manicured gel nails. If there was a garden in the restaurant's court-yard, I would have thought she had just come in from burying someone in it.

Raphael and Anna excused themselves before the Florentine Cake was served. While they had kissed and made up, I felt a festering storm of resentment was bubbling up under both their skins.

6

Waking to the sound of birds instead of traffic made me think for a moment I was back in Trasimeno. It took me some moments to realise I was in the centre of Florence beside the river Arno. A dream had woken me. I couldn't remember what it was about, but it was disturbing and my eyes immediately went to the trapdoor that interrupted the frescoed ceiling over near the ensuite. A large lock dangled from a crudely placed latch, keeping it shut tight.

I could sense Paolo was awake too. Without looking at him and still looking at the trapdoor, I asked, "What's up there?"

"I haven't been in that attic for years. Some of my mother's art stuff and a couple of boxes of books... oh and a table service from when Georgio's family had servants and big dinner affairs in the 1920s. I remember being up there as a kid and seeing the silver cloches."

"They probably would be worth some cash now on eBay. It might pay for their wedding." I was joking, trying to get Paolo to open up about yesterday's announcement. He didn't respond. Him lying still starring up at the four-poster canopy told me it still bothered him. I turned and leaned sideways on my elbow, looking at him.

"Did they discuss it with you over dinner?"

"They seem quite focused on it. And they want to do it soon, they're not hanging about." He still didn't move.

"How do you feel about it?"

"Well, it was a shock... he seems like a nice man... but there's something strange about the rush. It seems to be more of a practical thing for them rather than romantic. Although they seem very much in love. I'm coming around to the idea. They deserve to be happy, but I don't know... something is just not sitting right with me. I feel he's hiding something. It's probably me just being paranoid."

"Or the police officer in you is still surfacing..." I traced my finger around his chest hair, daring myself to ask the next question. "I'm curious... why did you leave the police force to become a hotel manager?"

"If I told you, I'd have to kill you," he smirked. "It's not a question suitable for a second date." He threw back the covers and rocked himself up into standing.

"We are not dating! I have told you, this is just a fling, so don't get too attached."

His Greek-god-like muscles on his tanned back made me breathe a little deeper as he walked around the bed to my side. "Well, whatever it is, I am definitely enjoying it. I am going for a shower. This is an old building and they like to conserve water. So I think I should insist that we shower together." He threw back the covers and scooped me up into his arms. I didn't protest.

Aunt Ciara was already up and had the breakfast table set for us when we finally made it out of the bedroom. She was in a silk emerald green robe and cream pyjamas with fluffy cream slippers, which I was sure were Versace.

"That's a big padlock you've got on the attic door. What are you hiding up there, Aunt Ciara? Dead bodies?" Paolo joked while having his typical Italian breakfast of just an espresso.

"That lock? I got it put on a few years ago. Actually, I wonder if you would go up and check the attic for me before you go? I heard a lot of movement up there a few weeks ago. I think there might be vermin or bats or something. Would you be a dear and check? I don't want to ask Valentino, as he has a bad hip and wouldn't be able to physically get up into the attic to check behind the boxes and stuff. I wouldn't want whatever it is up there chewing through the electric cables or your grandmother's stuff."

"Sure I will. I'll do it now if you like. Where do you keep your ladder?"

"Ladder? Hmm no... of course you will need a ladder, I hadn't thought of that." She laughed, getting up and moving to her more comfortable chair to where her notebook was.

"Maybe we could borrow one from that guy, Raphael?" I suggested pouring myself a cup of tea before clearing away the breakfast things.

"No, not him. He's way too nosy lately," said Aunt Ciara, snubbing out the idea with a face like she had a nasty taste in her mouth. "We could try Clive... The large, bald gentleman that was at the party, he lives in the first apartment on the far side of the courtyard."

"The guy sitting opposite Davide, that looks like a biker?" I walked out the open French doors on to the balcony where wisteria had arched over from the wrought-iron railing and spread its grip onto the frame built over one half of the large balcony creating a natural canopy to enjoy cool drinks under on warm summer days.

"That's him. An absolutely lovely chap. He gave up his position in the navy to nurse his mother for years. He's always so helpful, carries up any deliveries I need, fixed a dripping tap, buried Coco my cat in the garden when she died... A gentle giant, reminds me of George from *Of Mice and Men*."

"I'm not sure if that is a complimentary comparison, Aunt." Paolo called back as he joined me on the balcony and slid his arm around my waist. A rower glided by down below, cutting a shallow liquid valley into the Arno as he smoothly slid under the arches of the Ponte Vecchio.

"You know what I mean. Anyway, I am apologising in advance as I don't intend to be piling up jobs for you both while you are here but... as you are a wedding planner I'd really love if you could advise on the best place in the Uffizi for our wedding ceremony." I could hear the same tinkle of excitement in her voice as I hear from young brides calling me for the first time to discuss their wedding.

"Valentino has already spoken to them this morning and as we are both associates of the museum, they have said we can have our ceremony there, which would be so meaningful to us both." She joined us on the balcony, which still would comfortably have space for a few more people. "It will just be a small ceremony; the two of us, but we would like to do it sooner rather than later."

Paolo walked back inside. "I need another coffee." I did not yet know him well enough yet to read what he was thinking, but he still seemed disgruntled.

Aunt Ciara ignored him but continued to talk to me. "There is a chapel in the Pitti Palace. It's not open to the public, it's a small hidden secret alcove. I want nothing too fussy, so I would love a woman's opinion on it," she whispered, so no man in earshot would be offended. "And of course, as you are in the wedding business, you will know what is possible more than Valentino, bless him."

I couldn't help but reflect her gentle smile. It didn't matter their age; she was in love with her man and was doing all the tricks of making it a perfect day in her eyes, for both of them.

"Sure. Hidden secret rooms full of history and ghosts are right up my street. I haven't been at the Uffizi for a few years and I was hoping we could fit in a visit while here. How about today?"

"Splendid! I'll call Valentino now and see what time he can meet you. I won't go, if you don't mind. I'm quite exhausted after all of yesterday's excitement. I'll leave the decision of where is best to you."

"Paolo," I called into the kitchen, "Hurry and finish that coffee we are going to the Uffizi."

7

Most people go to the Uffizi Art Museum to look at the paintings. I go to look at the ceilings and the perfect view of the Ponte Vecchio from one of its window. Art museums seemed to be turning into a rendezvous habit between Paolo and I. Our last trip, or date as he likes to call it, was to the Sistine Chapel.

I had forgotten that in the Uffizi you start at the top and work your way down. I was glad I had chosen to wear my baggy cotton pants and Birkenstock sandals as my knees creaked going up the endless flights of wide stone stairs. But reaching my favourite spot—the long connecting gallery with the frescoed ceilings—made the effort worth it.

"They must have been on drugs of some kind, to come up with these weird creatures," I said, craning my neck back to look at some of the thousands of detailed bizarre and sometimes grotesque figures painstakingly painted on the long gallery's vaulted ceilings. Paolo didn't answer. He didn't answer because he was no longer by my side. He had ambled off by himself through the connecting dark wood rooms dripping with evocative masterpieces by Botticelli, Rembrandt, Michelangelo and da Vinci.

I had learnt from our last trip to the Vatican art galleries that he enjoyed viewing art in silence on his own. Whereas I liked discussion. Either discussing the art in front of me or to have the art as background viewing while discussing anything and everything.

After about an hour, we ended up in the same room as each other again. Amongst the hanging paintings I came across a discrete blank spot. There was a painting missing.

I waited for Paolo to amble across to be by my side before raising the alarm. "Paolo, someone has nicked a painting," I said in a loud whisper, so I wouldn't have to repeat myself. He casually looked around "Well, I can't see anyone with a suspicious rectangular shape under their coat and a swag bag in their hand."

"It has indeed been stolen from us," said a now familiar voice. It was Valentino coming up to my side to gaze at the blank space. He might have a crappy hip, but there was nothing wrong with his ears.

"You're here early," I chirped.

"Yes, I'm not one for sleeping late, so I often go for an early morning walk by the Arno and usually end up here working on something in the studios. I see you have found our blank space."

The three of us stood staring at the only wall spot in the Uffizi without artwork on it. It would have been a wonderful photo if someone had snapped us.

"It is a symbolic statement to try to get back the famous Vase of Flowers painting from Germany," explained Valentino.

"The painting you and Ciara have been trying to get back? Davide told Paolo and I about it yesterday. Is there any hope of it being returned?"

"There have been rumours recently that we are close, very close. The painting is still owned by the Italian State, and so it can be neither sold nor purchased, so that is a positive. We've made such a racket about it internationally, no underground dealer would touch it with a gondola pole."

Paolo migrated on to the next room while Valentino and I ambled along, side by side. His hands clasped behind his back. His white hair combed back and his perfectly groomed beard and perfectly tailored cream linen suit gave him a look of one of the older men out of *The Godfather* movies.

"There were so many works of art stolen for Hitler's Museum of Art he intended to build," he lamented. "And so many destroyed because Hitler did not like the style or did not want them to fall into the hands of the allies when the war was over. It would be just wonderful for Ciara and I to achieve getting even this one piece back before our life's work is over."

"Were none of the paintings they took saved or ever found?" I asked, standing in front of the magnificent Birth of Venus, where we found Paolo again.

"Oh yes. The Nazis stored 6,500 paintings, including works by Michelangelo, Vermeer and Rembrandt, in a salt mine in Austria with orders for it to be blown up if the allies won. It is believed local miners and a Nazi official, who swapped the vast bombs for smaller ones, thwarted the plan. So when they were detonated, they only brought down enough rubble to block the entrance. The works remained safe, underground, until the Monuments Men–an Allied task force charged with finding and saving Europe's art–got to them after the war ended. You may have seen the movie made about the task force, *The Monuments Men*?"

"No, I didn't. I am not much of a TV or movie buff. I don't give myself much time to relax, I'm all work and no play."

"You sound like Ciara. She is always working on some project. I think she is afraid that if she stops, she will just keel over. I am hoping I will help her take time out for herself."

Paolo had gone on ahead by himself again.

"Valentino, you may have noticed that Paolo is not yet too enamoured at the idea of his aunt getting married. Your work may be cut out for you with him."

"Yes indeed. But I think only time and my actions will get him on my side. Ciara tamed me a lot and made me feel true love again. It is not something I have felt for nearly 30 years. Since my wife Maria, God rest her, passed away." His voice dropped an octave and for the first time since I met him, his face was devoid of a smile.

"Anyway, we are not here to be gloomy, let me show you the Chapel and then we can have a drink on the roof terrace." He perked up as we wound our way around staircases and corridors, leaving Paolo lost in his happy place, surrounded by art.

Neither of us could have guessed what the next hour was to bring.

8

"**W**ow, it's very... full on." They were the only words that immediately found my lips when Valentino opened the doors to the sumptuous mix of red walls and curtains and the ornate gold ceiling of the tiny chapel. It definitely was not the simplicity Ciara was looking for.

"I know Ciara said the ceremony would just be the two of us, but I think she is just being kind to me. I don't like fuss, but she enjoys having friends around and a party, so I was thinking we could have a brunch after the ceremony, just a small group of about 30 to 50 people. There is a pleasant room down in the restoration studios where we could have it, I think. Just something simple. I'll show it to you, but let's have a drink first."

'Simple.' That word always made me uneasy when someone used it to describe the wedding they wanted, thinking it would make it less expensive. "Hay bales for chairs, and candles dotted around the lawn, just something simple like that," was a common request for a few years, thanks to Pinterest. It would take me a while to explain that getting hay bales to a location was a lot more difficult than hiring in chairs. And that it would take hundreds of candles to achieve the effect they were after. They all had to be in some sort of dish or lantern to ensure they didn't get blown out and someone had to light each individual candle, which would take two hours, which meant taking on another staff member just to look after the candles.

While Valentino wasn't talking about hay bales and candles, he hadn't had put much thought into his idea of something simple. I broke into a sweat on the way to the museum's roof terrace, watched over by Palazzo Vecchio's clock face tower. Not because of the many stone steps, it was the thought of the week ahead. The last-minute simple wedding I had agreed to organise was turning into a full-on affair. It didn't matter whether it was 30 or people, it still meant finding a caterer, organising menus, seating plans, guest dietary needs, music, furniture, linens, table arrangements, staff. Of course, Valentino wasn't thinking about this. He was just thinking of keeping the new love of his life happy.

We found Paolo on the terrace having an early Aperol Spritz. If I was a cat, the hairs would have been standing up on the arch of my back at this point. He was not only being sulky about his Aunt's decision to get married but was now leaving me to be the gracious one, running around after his aunt's fiancé while he sat in the sun having a cocktail. Not only that, but I had somehow been rigged into planning a complimentary wedding for two strangers at breakneck speed. While he was having a bloody cocktail! And this was all happening on my week off, after he got me here under the guise of a romantic week away. My chest was tightening and my joints were becoming more rigid. My sweating over Valentino's simpleness was turning into anger at Paolo's flippant-ness.

Valentino continued on as if our conversation hadn't been interrupted by him stopping off to get me a cappuccino while I sat giving Paolo the silent treatment, without him realising it.

"The room I am thinking of is one of the rooms where Filippo and I teach students the first elements of restoration techniques and where Filippo does the odd exclusive art lesson for tour groups with big pockets. I've just seen Filippo at the coffee counter so he will bring you down to the room as I just have had an urgent call down to the office which I must attend to. I'll catch up with you in the room, but now I must dash."

With that, a short, well-built, bald guy in a crisp blue shirt walked towards our table, passing Valentino on the way between tables. They exchanged a quick few words and Valentino pointed him in our direction. With every step towards us, his shoulders twitched as he cleared his throat twice. "I'm Filippo Garcia. Valentino asked me to join you."

"Yes, please do," said Paolo, half standing to greet him with a handshake as Filippo placed his double espresso on the table and pulled out a chair. Smears of white and pale blue paint were bedded into his cuticles and the hard skin surrounding his nails. It seemed to be permanent, a part of him that no amount of scrubbing would remove.

"I hear we are going to have a wedding. I have never heard of two people getting married so old. It's funny." He laughed a little at his own words while rocking slightly in his chair.

I don't think he meant it as insulting, but that is the way it sounded. His eye contact was fleeting, so he didn't pick up Paolo's raised eyebrows reaction. "My aunt is young at heart and they are not stupid..."

Wow, he was actually defending Valentino, at least that was some progress.

"So, you teach here?" I asked, changing the subject.

"Yes, I have been here ten years. Before that I was in Russia restoring art works for the Imperial painting collection at the Old Russian Painting Conservation Studio." His chest expanded with this boast and his awkwardness in our company diminished with it.

"So you must know Natasha... I can't remember her second name..."

"Natasha Verbotski," stated Filippo.

"Yes, that's her. I met her at Ciara's birthday dinner yesterday. Interesting woman." I added before recalling too late that Raphael had jibbed at Natasha about Filippo, and she had insulted his artistic talent in some way.

"Yes, I know Natasha, we were... together... for a while, when she lived here. She's one of those women who loves you madly one minute and would slit your throat the next." He directed his last sentence at Paolo, as if he, as a fellow male version of our species, would completely understand what he meant about passionate woman slitting people's throats. Paolo nodded slowly in agreement while fiddling mindlessly with the spoon on his saucer.

"Shall we go to see the room? I am just aware that it will be lunch time shortly and I don't want to keep you from your break." I urged. I didn't care about his lunch. I was just tired of having formal conversations and I wasn't going to go down the tunnel of where this conversation was leading. Paolo's behaviour so far this morning had him tethered on the 'nice knowing you' wall with a possible push into the land of past boyfriends. I wanted some quiet time alone to wander the streets of Florence, visit the food market, eat gelato and people watch before I had to launch into a pronto wedding for the rest of the week.

"Okay let's go," Filippo said, knocking back the remains of his coffee while we all screeched the legs of our wrought-iron chairs on the paving stones.

Filippo led the way down the 'staff only' back stairs. "So do you have a class today?" I asked, continuing to make polite conversation for as long as was needed, while my head was already planning the streets I wanted to get lost in.

"Yes actually. It starts in about 15 minutes. Do either of you paint?"

"I used to," piped up Paolo. "I had some paintings in an exhibition in Venice once, but then my life took a different direction. Someday I'll get back to it."

I looked back at Paolo, two or three steps behind me. "You never cease to surprise me. First the police force and now you were a painter too?"

"Police force?" splurged out Filippo, pausing for a moment on his step and taking the handrail. "You are in the Carabinieri?" He looked like he would shortly need smelling salts. He was definitely more shocked at the news of Paolo being in the police force than I was at Paolo being a painter.

"*Was* in the police force. I am no longer. I am now a hotel manager for the Russi chain of hotels. It's a lot more relaxing than the police force. There is less potential of being killed."

"Be careful not to speak too soon Paolo. You have no idea how annoying hotel managers can be, to overworked wedding planners," I casually said. Paolo shot a what-have-I-done-to-deserve-that look in my direction. If I had a tail, I would have swished it walking down the stairs behind Filippo, as Paolo caught up after being stopped in his tracks by my deadly word attack. At last, he knew I was annoyed with him.

"I'll be with you all shortly, I just need to fix up the easels and show these people the room," said Filippo to the four mature students already waiting outside the door of the studio. Two looked up and nodded from their phone screens, another two were leaning on the windowsill, too absorbed in sketching to have heard what Filippo said.

The room surprised me. Yes, with the easels moved, the clutter in the corners gone and the partition screen and furniture behind it cleared away, the room would easily fit one hundred people. But there was absolutely nothing special, unless they were looking for a seventies-style classroom vibe for their wedding, which I don't think Ciara had in mind.

"There are much nicer rooms, but this is one of our bigger rooms, so I suppose that is why Valentino choose it. Here I'll clear this and you can imagine the size of it better," said Filippo apologetically.

Just as Filippo was pushing back the screen partition, a familiar voice bellowed from the doorway behind us, "This isn't the room I meant Filippo, it was studio five...." I turned to see Valentino standing in the doorway. His eye's wide, mouth a gape, his knuckles whitening as he gripped the half-open door and door frame on the other side. I followed his line of vision. Everything was going in slow motion. I could see why his voice was lost, his last words cut short at the sight behind the folded back screen.

A semi-naked woman was lying perfectly posed on a chaise lounge, her long black hair falling over the curved blue velvet arm. A pool of blood glistened in the sun, having dripped from her garroted neck.

9

S tepping back, I found the wall to steady myself against. I was
unable to breathe, grabbing my lips to capture the ball of air that
contained a scream. It was enclosed tight in my fist. I glanced towards
the door. Valentino was in the room, plastered against the now closed
door. Paolo had immediately rushed to the girl. He was beside her on
bended knee, holding her limp hand in his as if proposing to her.
Filippo had fallen backwards onto the floor, slipping in the crimson
pool as he went.

"Oh Dio, it's Julia Svoboda," Valentino was squeezing both his cheeks
with one hand as if to keep his jaw disintegrating while meeting
Filipo's wide eyes with his own.

"She's dead... murdered," confirmed Paolo, shocked but with the
solemn tone of a police officer telling someone their wife had died in
a car accident. "We need to cordon off the area." He already had his
phone to his ear, standing, careful not to disturb anything around.

"You'll need to take off your shoes and leave them here," he instructed
Filippo, pointing at his now bloodied sole. "Nobody touch anything in
the room, including the doors and walls." Paolo instructed as he

waited on the phone line to be put through to the person he had requested to speak to. Both Valentino and I twitched a little at the thought of moving away from the secure positions our bodies had velcroed themselves to.

"Filippo, when you get a grip of yourself, I want you to go out to the students and calmly tell them there is no class today. Do not tell them about what has happened. The four of us need to stay in the room until the police get here and evaluate the scene. So if you would all be so kind to move to the chairs near the window, I will give the victim her discretion and move the screen back to where it was." I could hear the crackling hold music in his earpiece from where I was standing. I could not see her face, but the scene in front of us looked like a depiction of some of the paintings we had just seen in the gallery.

"Valentino. Will you please take the seat over there?" Paolo instructed calmly. Valentino, for the first time in my visit, looked old, old and suction cupped to where he was standing. He didn't look well. I was afraid for a moment that he was having a stroke or a heart attack. I didn't want two fatalities on our hands. Although a speeding thought fast tracked through my cynical head, about how I wouldn't have to plan a wedding at short notice if he died on the spot. I went and took his elbow and guided him over to the window.

"Hello, Emanuele. Yes, it is Paolo Ferrari... Yes, we have not seen each other in sometime..." Paolo was squeezing his forehead like he was trying to soften putty. I could tell he was waiting for a space to say why he was calling to the enthusiastic inspector on the other end of the phone.

"Yes, I am in town at the moment, visiting from Rome, but that's not why I'm calling. You need to come to the art studios of the Uffizi as soon as you can. There has been a murder. The victim is a woman in her late 20s she's been dead several hours. There is no suspect at the scene. I was here when the body was discovered in a private room. I am closing off the area. It's on the first floor, in the restoration studios." Paolo was talking down the phone, just like I've heard them do at the scene of a crime in cop movies. No sentiment, just plain facts.

"Valentino Bruni, the professor in charge, is here with me. The teacher of the class and... a friend of mine is here too. We were all here when the body was discovered... Yes, we will wait for you." His call ended just as I sat down beside Filippo and Valentino. Filippo had his head in his hands.

"She's a life model here, part time. She has worked here at the studios for about three years. I better go tell the students there will be no class today." Filippo lifted his head and looked ahead to the door as if he was an Olympic swimmer looking to the end of the pool while waiting for the start whistle. His knees creaked a little as he stood up and then walked close to the wall in his stocking feet, giving the screen and scene behind it as wide a berth as possible. The police car sirens could already be heard in the distance.

"Is there a studio we can get the students to wait in? The police will need to ask them some questions, to see if they saw anything suspicious," said Paolo, walking to the door with Filippo. "Yes, of course. I will tell them to wait in studio five for me. I will just say we cannot use this room... as there has been an accident." He was thinking on his stockinged feet.

Suddenly, the door opened wide. "What's happening here? You all look like you have seen a ghost." Raphael was standing at the door. "I've just come to pick up Julia has anyone seen her?" Paolo was already beside the door and in the seconds it took Raphael to have opened the door and say the words, Paolo had shuffled his and Filippo's movements like he was splitting a deck of cards, moving Raphael firmly in with his arm around his shoulder and projecting Filippo out to his students through the narrowest opening possible in the door with his other hand, shutting the door after him. The police car sirens were getting closer.

. . .

"Oh my! Is that blood?" pointed Raphael.

Valentino immediately responded, "It's Julia, she has been murdered."

Filippo squeezed himself back into the room and closed the door after himself. "Why did you push me out? I am sure they are all now wondering why I am not wearing shoes."

"Oh my... who would do such a thing to Julia." Raphael was becoming hysterical. We could hear him over the police and ambulance sirens, which were pulling into the courtyard below. His fingers were clawed and both sets of digits were in his thick, black hair, like he was going to give himself a firm head massage.

He grabbed on to the partition screen and looked behind "Mamma Mia."

As soon as Paolo caught up with him, Paolo landed his hands firmly on Raphael's shoulders and stopped him thrashing around the room like a wind-up toy having just been released from the hands of a child.

"Please take a seat Raphael, you are in the room now, so you need to stay until the police get here. We can't have you scattering your DNA around everywhere." The hysterical Raphael gripped onto Paolo, then reeled around on his heel, eyes rolling back into his head and slammed up against the wall, face forward, his arms splayed, blubbering.

"Please Raphael, you must sit down and contain yourself," said Valentino, walking over and assisting Paolo by taking a firm grip of his flailing arms. Raphael deflated like a burst blow-up doll. Paolo released him into the care of Valentino's grip and went to the door. A drumroll of boots on the internal stone steps down the hall could be heard, before a solemn , suited, bald striking looking man walked into the room behind Paolo followed by a guy with a camera, three police officers and a woman wearing a clinical white coat, large glasses and her hair in a bun.

Courteous handshakes and words were exchanged between Paolo and what seemed like an old friend of his. He then led the detective to the screen where he had a quick glance, before he immediately instructed a fellow detective to question the students waiting in the other studio.

Paolo then led him over to us.

"This is Detective Marella, he'll want to talk to us all before we leave the room," said Paolo, taking a seat beside me.

"Thank you for waiting. I'll make this as quick as possible. Which of you discovered the body?" Detective Marella asked, taking a notebook out of his pocket with a pen attached to it by elastic.

"It was a few of us. Paolo, Daisy and I came into the room and..." said Filippo.

"Why did you come into the room?"

"I was viewing it for a wedding..." I chipped in.

"For a wedding in here? Of all the beautiful places in Florence, you were going to choose this room for your wedding?" he said, forgetting himself.

"Actually, it's for my wedding and it was the wrong room." Butted in Valentino. "Filippo was supposed to bring them to the room down the hall. It has better light and a nicer view, it's just for drinks and brunch after a small ceremony."

Marella was now eyeing up Valentino suspiciously, but for the wrong reason.

"*You* are getting married?" He rocked back and forth on his heels to toes. There was no wedding band on his finger. Did I hear a sense of disbelief mixed with a little jealousy?

"Yes, actually I am," confirmed Valentino, a little indignantly.

The detective's gaze lingered on Valentino for a moment longer and then it moved on to Raphael. "And you?"

"Oh, I wasn't here," said Raphael, somewhat relieved not to be associated with our criminal bunch.

"Why did you come in here?" he said, flicking open his notebook.

"Me? I was collecting Julia, to bring her to my fiancé Anna's apartment for lunch. They are good friends... were good friends... from the same town in the Czech Republic." Raphael bit his bottom lip before dropping his head onto his fist. "Poor Anna... poor Julia."

This didn't quite make sense to me, didn't Anna call Julia a bitch the night before and say 'she is no friend of mine' to Raphael, 'more your friend now'? Perhaps there was something going on between Raphael and the murdered woman. Perhaps Anna had a right to be annoyed at him. Or perhaps he had persuaded her to make up with her friend and have lunch together.

"Did anyone else here know the deceased?"

"Yes," echoed Filippo and Valentino.

"She works here as a life drawing model, so we have both known her three or four years."

"Did you see anyone leave the room before you came in or did you see anything suspicious in the hallways around?"

Everyone just shrugged or shook their head.

"Is there anyone you know of that would have reason to kill her?"

It was then Filippo looked at Raphael, Raphael looked at Valentino, Valentino looked at Filippo. The silence said it all to me. Either they knew something, or one of them killed her.

10

After some more questions and contact details taken, we were free to go.

I waited outside, eavesdropping at the ajar door. My hearing is excellent I can just about hear a pin drop three rooms away. I could see Detective Marella's lips enough to read them.

"Look at this Paolo..." said the detective, crouched behind the chaise longue. "This looks like mud residue around the neck wound."

Paolo glanced across to the door where I was staring in through the crack. I stepped back, but it was too late. He had seen me. I know he probably would have told me all the details later, so it was embarrassing to be caught snooping.

"I'm going to stick around here for a while to help Emanuele, I mean Detective Marella, until forensics and the coroner get here... We know each other from my days in the police force," Paolo said, explaining their obvious bond.

"Of course... I'm just waiting on Valentino to get his things from the other room and I'll walk back with him to your Aunt's. He seems quite shaken still," I say, a bit flustered from the embarrassment of being caught.

"And you? Are you okay?" Paolo put his hand gently on my arm, his brown eyes filled with genuine concern.

"I'm fine. Just in shock, I suppose. I've never seen something like that before." His gentleness had softened my hard exterior and made me vulnerable to the rising emotions.

Thankfully, Valentino appeared with his coat over his arm. His shuffling feet echoed through the quietened hallways. All the studios had been evacuated by the police and closed for the day until forensics had their way with the rooms.

"Would you like to stop for a coffee?" I asked Valentino on the way out to the street where people were doing normal things. Laughing, taking selfies, buying trinkets from the souvenir booths, unaware that a woman had been murdered just behind the walls of where they stood.

"I think something stiffer would be better," he responded, taking my arm as we walked down the wheelchair ramp and made our way across the cobbles.

At a bar on Piazza della Signoria, he had drunk his second caffe corretto–an espresso with a shot of brandy–before I approached the subject.

"Did you know her well?"

He fiddled with his saucer, turning it around as if it was something that had to be done before he could speak. It's at times like this that I miss Shadow being near. Everyone found petting her floppy ears a comfort in times of need and she was the perfect height to put her head on your lap and give a loving comforting look with her big golden eyes.

"Julia was a wonderful woman. She had an energy about her that was contagious. Before she came here, the studios were more silent. Just places of work and not much interaction. When she arrived, she brought a whirlwind with her. A passion, a reminder not to take life too seriously. There's laughter and emotion now, a different level of bonding and kinship amongst the staff. I put all down to Julia and Anna... but mostly Julia. I can't imagine why someone would do such a thing." His gaze was on the statue of Donatello's Judith and Holofernes, where the woman of marble stood holding the slain Holofernes by the hair, after slitting his throat.

"It's probably not the best choice of place to stop for a coffee with all this gruesomeness staring at us," I said, looking towards Loggia della Signoria with its displays of colossal marble statues depicting scenes from classical history where women were not coming out the best; Perseus holding up the head of Medusa, The Rape of Polyxena, The Rape of Sabine and with all the Vestal Virgins watching.

Valentino contemplated, "I find them comforting. Many are stories of hope and strength of women which tend to be missed sometimes. The strong over the weak."

As we walked back to the apartment, my mind had drifted back to the studio. To the way Julia's body lay across the chaise longue in the translucent, long white nightdress. It had looked like something from a period drama, a string of pearls falling from her hand. Her outfit was not something a woman would go for a walk to the store in.

"Was Julia working with students yesterday?"

"I don't know. I had taken a few days off to prepare for the party, but generally on Sundays, there are no classes. Often she went in to work on her own ceramic work on Sundays and on her days off... I never saw her working on stuff. She liked to keep it to herself, but she and Anna often worked all day at the studios. Although I haven't seen them together for quite some time."

As we rounded onto the pathway along the Arno, I had an urge to break away from Vincenzo's linked arm and make a run for it down one of the meandering cobbled streets that I so wanted to get lost in. Browse the antique shops, buy some Florentine handmade gift-wrap paper. I already had a whole selection of it at home in Trasimeno, all too nice to use. Perhaps this time I would find a trinket in one of the ancient side-street shops that specialised in mirrors, globes or carnivale papier mache masks, to wrap up for Sophia. Or perhaps I would just get her the usual fridge magnet gift I got her everywhere I went because she hated them so much. It didn't matter what I bought for her; it was just going to be an excuse for me to buy a sheet or several sheets of beautiful paper.

But having just been at the scene of a murder and with a still shaken Vincenzo on my arm, the secret streets and papermill shops would have to wait until another time. Perhaps if I helped figure out who did it, I could have even an afternoon free to myself without guilt.

"Anna is Raphael's fiancé, right? I met her at the party yesterday. She didn't seem too fond of Julia."

"Oh, don't mind Anna, she and Julia were always bickering about something, hot-blooded Eastern Europeans!"

"But she seemed quite... jealous."

"Anna doesn't hold back telling people what she thinks. Neither did Julia. They both came here to study ceramics and funded their studies as artists' models. Julia tended to get more work. She had more of a classical look. A fuller, more voluptuous figure with long black hair and seductive eyes. She was often compared to Adele Bloch-Bauer—a friend of the artist Gustav Klimt whom he often used as a subject for his paintings."

"Oh Klimt, I'm a big fan. I saw his 'Kiss' in Vienna."

"Yes, yes, I am a big fan too. The Nazis destroyed a lot of his work when they were retreating unfortunately. Thirteen of his pieces were being stored in the castle Schloss Immendorff in Austria, which they blew up. The tragic thing was that they, along with other art, were originally placed in the castle for safekeeping until the war was over. There were so many tragedies beyond measure."

"But Julia, if she wasn't at the studio working, then why was she there... like that... I mean, she was clearly posing for a portrait, wasn't she?"

"Yes, I suppose she was." Valentino was distracted, searching in his pocket for the key to the street door into Ciara's apartment courtyard, and eventually found it in his inside jacket pocket.

"Did she model for many artists other than the students?"

"She used to. She was very popular amongst the artist community. Often, they lavished her with gifts. I bet that is where the pearls came from. And, of course, she posed at the Uffizi studios."

I was running through the conversation I had had with Anna and Raphael at the party. Anna had said he was more Julia's friend now, and he had said they were working on something together.

"Other than the art classes at the Uffizi, do you know who she posed for there?" To me this was purely a qualifying question. I felt I already had this mystery figured out, but the answer was not who I was expecting.

"Only Filippo now, I think. They were having an affair, he's a very protective sort, and I heard he didn't approve of her posing for anyone else. But before you go thinking things, he's a silent type. He wouldn't do something so grotesque as what we saw. He was very protective of her." With a key wiggle in the lock, the door clicked loudly.

"It's sometimes the quiet ones you have to watch," I mumbled. But Vincenzo was not paying attention to what I had to say any longer. He was too distracted about getting to the apartment and seeing Ciara before she heard the news.

The creak of the heavy door opening drowned out the next thoughts I voiced to him. "And was he protective... or jealous?"

11

Back at the apartment, Aunt Ciara was lying stretched out on the long wide sofa sleeping in the chinked, wisteria-shaped shadows, shimmering through the balcony doors.

Valentino crept to her side and gently covered her with the light cashmere blanket that had slid off onto the parquet floor. He removed his shoes and followed me quietly into the kitchen where I was pouring myself a glass of chardonnay left over from the party, "Waste not want not, would you like a glass?" I said as he entered.

"I do need to take my medication, but let's have a glass together anyway as there is something I would like to discuss," he said, easing himself into the armchair in the corner near the kitchen window.

"The reason I had to rush off this morning and leave you in the care of Filippo was because the Lord Mayor was in my office. She's a good friend of ours and was at the party yesterday. Perhaps you were not introduced? Anyway, when she was leaving last night Ciara and I asked her to check when was the soonest possible date we could get married. After checking her diary and the permissions waiver because of our age, she is willing to do it on Thursday... Can you help make it happen on Thursday?"

"THURSDAY?? This week?"

"Yes. Yes. I know it's very short notice, but we can go back to the idea of just the two of us, no big fuss. Today made me realise I want to marry Ciara more than ever, as soon as possible. I know what we experienced today was very unpleasant, and I didn't get to show you the room I was speaking about for the brunch after the ceremony but I would like us to push ahead and get married this week."

"You'll need two witnesses to make it legal." My head was beginning to hurt, not just from the pressure but from the alcohol top-ups too early in the day.

"You and Paolo could do that role, couldn't you?"

"Let's wait and speak with Ciara and figure things out." The front bell buzzed, causing us both to jerk.

"Coming!" Ciara called out, her voice still muffled with sleep.

"It's okay, I'll get it!" I called out, walking into the hall.

"Daisy, you are back!" said Ciara, sitting herself upright on the sofa. On the CCTV, I could see it was Paolo outside. I pressed the buzzer to let him in, although I felt like leaving him out there a little longer to think about what he had done. Murder or no murder, I was still annoyed with him for his earlier behaviour.

"Is Valentino with you?" Ciara called after me. "I have been trying to call both him and Paolo-"

"Yes, I am back sweetheart." Valentino had new life in his voice, forgetting the grave past few hours.

"So you have heard the news?" Ciara seemed ecstatic. Too happy to be talking about a murder. Valentino hadn't noticed her joyous tone. He was concentrating on not spilling the cup of chai tea he was carrying out of the kitchen to his beloved.

"It is dreadfully sad," Valentino became grim again while taking her hands and helping her stiff joints ease to standing so she could join us at the table.

Paolo closed the front door softly behind him. His face was dour and close to looking grey even though it was warm out. I felt my limbs and heart soften towards him. It had been a tough morning.

"What do you mean, Valentino? How can the return of The Vase of Flowers be sad? Oh no... have they destroyed it?" Ciara was on the verge of falling over with the thought she had just manifested.

"Ciara, what did you just say?" said Valentino. "They are returning The Vase of Flowers?"

"YES! Natasha called. I've been trying to call you to tell you the news! I thought with you being over at the gallery someone would have found you to tell you."

"Emm no, we were busy with... something else... but this is great news sweetheart. When will it be arriving, have they said?"

"They have already prepared it for transportation. It arrives on Thursday," enthused Ciara.

"Oohh... That is the day I was hoping we could get married. We have got approval from the town hall, and they have a slot available on Thursday afternoon."

Watching the two of them was like watching 20-year-olds talking about an exciting concert that coincided with one of their best friend's birthdays. It was time for me to intervene and share the sparks going off in my head.

"I've an idea," I piped up, taking Paolo's hand and stepping into the lounge.

"Instead of the chapel, why don't you have your wedding vows in front of The Vase of Flowers after it has been revealed? I'm sure you have been staring at that blank space on the gallery wall as longingly as you have been staring at each other for the last few years."

They both looked at each other with the biggest grins and softest eyes. It was a scene too gorgeous, and for some reason my throbbing head felt the need to break it.

"The good thing is you will save money on flower decoration. And the gallery will surely be supplying a drinks reception for the big reveal, so that will save money too and all your friends from the committee will be there, so hey, it murders so many birds with the one fragmented stone." The translation from English to Italian obviously hadn't worked too well.

Valentino was looking a little horrified at me. Paolo was looking bemused by my ill-fitting choice of words, considering the situation we had all just experienced. Ciara was just her joyous self.

"It's all such a good idea, but the only issue is... they always said I would have a big role in the organising of the welcome home event and reveal of the painting if we ever got it back. The gallery will have a PR and security team working on the painting reveal, but I expected this to happen when I was younger, not so suddenly and not on my wedding day. It's all too much work Valentino. I am sorry we will have to postpone the wedding, and I think I need to hand the role over to someone else on the committee to organise the reveal. "

"I won't hear of that," Valentino said. "It is the perfect day for us to celebrate everything we love. The painting and each other." He turned to me. "Daisy will help us make it happen. If we hand it to someone else, they may not allow us to say our vows, but if we are involved, then I don't think anyone can stop us."

This was no longer a wedding, it was a challenge. And I loved a challenge. "I would be happy to organise and co-ordinate both events but on one condition...."

They both blinked like rabbits in headlights. "My dog can come stay here."

"Of course, I love dogs."

I don't know if she realised what she was getting herself into as I scanned the room and mentally labelled eight objects, including a large antique Japanese vase, a ceramic sculpture and a cream velvet armchair that would need to be removed from the room before Shadow's destructive wagging tale and long black shedding hair arrived. But Ciara had agreed. There was no going back now.

I was already texting Sophia: "Wedding emergency, I need you and Shadow in Florence by this evening to arrange a wedding for Thursday."

Within minutes Sophia responded: "On it. Send me parking details for Vivienne Van, an outline and a list of what you need me to bring from the cantina within the next 30 minutes. Packing as we speak."

"Well Signora Ciara, it is time for you to find your wedding dress." I announced, all the annoyance about the last-minute organising of a wedding on my break had melted away. "I have called in my reinforcements. We will have you married in no time."

"I can't believe it. This is all fantastic. Now let's make a nice cup of tea and you can all tell me all about your lovely afternoon at the gallery."

A foggy silence fell on the room.

"I have a wedding to arrange, so I'll leave it to you guys," I said quickly. The three people in front of me were all going to be family soon. I was just an outsider brought along as a plus one to a party and was now working my socks off during my week off to make a lifetime memory happen for them. I didn't mind anymore. I was wearing my wedding hat again and looking forward to the challenge. I'd be damned if I was also going to be part of the whole drama of telling the bride that someone had been murdered at her wedding venue. I had already successfully avoided having to do this at another wedding in Rome at the start of the season. Coincidently it was when I bumped into Paolo again after not seeing him for three years.

"I also have a banging headache. So I'm going to take some time out in our room to plan the wedding and rest my head a bit. You guys can explain to Ciara where we have been this afternoon. She may want to change the wedding plans because of it."

I could nearly read the thoughts being fired back and forth between Paolo's and Valentino's eyes. "You're the cop, you tell her." "No, you are the one who wants to be her husband, you tell her." They were bonding in their awkwardness.

"Paolo, be a pet and bring me in a cuppa when you get a chance." I didn't wait for a response as I grabbed my laptop bag and scooted into the bedroom. I was glad to be focusing on solving a wedding dilemma rather than solving a murder mystery. Although I still felt solving the mystery would help make the wedding planning smoother.

12

I called Sophia's number as soon as I had closed the bedroom door behind me. I needed some friendly female company and some sense of normality. But she didn't answer. I guessed she was down in the cantina of Brigid Borgo, making random assumptions about things we might need for our sudden wedding.

It was probably just as well that she didn't answer as I would have, of course, spent the entire time talking about finding the body. Instead, I decided to skip telling her about the murder until she was here. We needed to focus on the wedding.

A few moments later Sophia texted: "Can't answer at the moment, just jumping into the shower. Text me a rundown and what I need to bring."

"So here's a rundown; The bride is 80, the groom is 75," I texted.

"Ok, so she's got herself a toy boy," was her response.

"Ceremony will be in the Uffizi and I am going to suggest a reception in their favourite local trattoria, if we can get it booked." Although Valentino had gone back to the idea of it being just the two of them, I still felt they would want their friends to get together after the ceremony. I continued to text Sophia the plans as I worked through them in my head:

"No chairs needed. It will be a quick standing ceremony. But perhaps we should have two on standby as the couple are elderly... I'll check the chairs available at the Uffizi but if there is nothing suitable, Ciara, the bride, lives close by and has some very nice antique chairs we can get brought over.

"No decoration nor table needed for the ceremony. However, bring the roll of chiffon, and all the string of lights and three boxes of pillar candles of three different sizes. I haven't seen the inside of the trattoria so I want to be prepared if it needs a bit of sprucing up.

"We need a bouquet for the bride and two boutonnieres (groom and best man)--these should be based on The Vase of Flowers. Call Davide about this, he'll know what I am talking about.

"No transport needed, as everything is within walking distance of each other.

"Hair and makeup–I'll need to check with the bride what she would like. She probably knows someone local she uses, so no action needed on this yet.

"Speeches and Toasts–we may need a mic if necessary in the trattoria. So bring along the mobile speaker and mic. Although being Italian, they will probably won't do speeches, just toasts.

"So that's all for now. I hope to see you in a couple of hours. You wouldn't believe what happened today. This summer is turning out to be the oddest wedding season ever."

As soon as I hit send, I put my phone to the side, got my pen and my latest pretty notebook out of my bag, and sank my back into the feather pillows on the bed. Nothing compares to a pen and paper when working on a to-do list and there is nothing more satisfying than ticking-off done 'to-dos'.

To dos;

Check with restaurant and book it for dinner on Thursday: Me

Contact Davide regarding flowers: Sophia

Contact Lord Mayor and confirm paperwork details for the wedding: Me with Valentino

Contact PR company of Uffizi and find out when will the media call be finished: Me

Get outline of what the timeline is for the big reveal: Me

Meet with head of security and establish a procedure for the big reveal: Me

Check guest list for reveal event to ensure all their friends are included: Me

Check if they will have music for the reveal, if not book a string quartet to play during ceremony and at the restaurant: Me... ask Ciara for the contact of the musicians that were at her party.

Find a photographer: Sophia

Agree a menu and wines: Me

Book a cake: Sophia

Hair and makeup: Check with Ciara.

Just as I was finished, I heard a soft knock. My eyes shot to the attic door. The lock was gone. Immediately, the dream I had forgotten came flooding back. A girl in a white dress, similar to the one Julia was wearing, with long black hair tied back with a large satin bow, pale skin, ruddy cheeks and dark eyes banging on the other side of the attic door. It was like my soul had drifted up into the attic and I was watching her trying to get out. She just looked up at me and mouthed some words I couldn't understand.

The knock happened again. I released my fear-held breath. It was coming from the door. "Are you sleeping?" said Ciara's voice gently.

"No, no, come in," I called like lady Muck on my four poster, velvet-strewn bed.

She had changed into a long, burnt-orange kaftan with large white lilies printed on it. Her silver hair had been released and its confinement in the bun had created waves in her hair that bounced on her shoulders.

"My goodness, the boys told me about what happened at the studio. That poor girl. And how awful for you all to experience that."

"It was quite a shock, but thankfully Paolo was there and took charge of the scene. How is Valentino doing? I think he was quite shocked."

"He's okay now," she said, coming over to sit on the side of my bed.

"Did you know Anna too?"

"I don't know the girl, but... I had heard of her." Ciara was looking at her fingernails.

"Are you okay to still go ahead with the wedding on Thursday? I mean, it's a nice idea doing it on the same day the painting returns, but we can wait if you prefer?"

While I had already switched into wedding mode, if Ciara had said they had decided to postpone, I would still have been happy to escape back to my vegetable patch in Trasimeno. Sure, why wouldn't she? Everyone else seemed to be catching on to the trend of postponing weddings that year.

"No no no, let's do it. I want Paolo to be there and God only knows when he will get time off again. Also, at our age, why wait?"

As if on cue, Paolo came into the room carrying the long-awaited cup of tea.

"How are you doing, has your headache eased?" He was being his lovely caring self again.

"Yes thanks, the painkillers seem to be doing their job. What happened after we left, any clues of who done it?"

"Well, they had Filippo in for questioning. It transpired that him and the victim were an item and he was quite... protective of her."

There was that word again. Protective. From what I had learned so far about Julia, she sounded perfectly capable of protecting herself. Except, perhaps, from someone overcome with jealousy strangling her.

"They have let him go but they are now taking Anna down to the police station for questioning."

"Anna? The girl at dinner?" I thought back to her snarky comments about Julia.

And then it clicked just before Paolo said it; her fingernails. The muddy residue on the victim's neck. "Was Julia killed by a potter's wire? Anna and Julia did ceramics together on the weekends, didn't they?"

Paolo nodded.

"That is awful. Do they truly think she did it?" Without even realising it, beside my to-do list, I was scribbling down the names of possible culprits. Filippo, Anna.

"They are only talking to her at the moment. It means nothing. And Anna and Raphael were at the party."

"That alibi won't wash as they left early...." said Ciara.

"We had all left the restaurant before the time the murdered happened. And everyone at the dinner was in the vicinity of the crime scene and most have a key. They will probably want to talk to anyone who was at the party who had a key to the studios."

Something didn't sit right for me with this whole scenario. "But it makes little sense. Julia was dressed and ready to pose for a modelling session... like a classical painting."

Ciara was still sitting on the bed, fiddling with her ring on her middle finger. Her ring finger was bare but thinned in the middle of the joint closer to her hand. There had been a ring on it for 50 years before her last husband died. Paolo had told me about him on the way to Florence. She looked sad. This bride needed to get back to being excited about her wedding. "Ciara," I said, pulling her attention back into the room. "How about you and I organise dinner together and start planning this wedding, I have a tonne of questions."

Her dimples reappeared. "I'll put the water on for the pasta. The caterers left a tonne of food in the fridge after the party which we need to use up. Paolo, you can get cleaned up. I'm sure you want to get changed and shake off all that bad feeling. I know I would."

13

While making dinner, I realised Ciara was going to be the perfect bride. She wanted everything fuss free, loved my ideas about the trattoria and everything else. We had the whole wedding planned by the time I was setting the table for dinner. "I think I even know the dress I am going to get. There's a small boutique on the other side of the river that had the most darling lace dress in the window only two weeks ago. It was so unusual I went in and asked about it. If it is still there, I will get it. It's handmade lace from an island on Lake... I can't remember which lake she said now."

"Lake Trasimeno?"

"Ah yes, that's it. How did you know?"

"It's where I live. Not on the island, in a small town on the lake shore."

"Ah yes, I remember Paolo mentioning that you were from Trasimeno. Have you ever been to the island?"

"Yes, I know the ladies who make the lace. There are only 15 left now living on the island. It's actually Irish lace they create. There's even an Irish lace museum there."

"Well, I never! What a coincidence in so many ways! I wonder how they came about making Irish lace in such an obscure place!"

"The story goes..." I said, putting down the tea towel I had used to dry the pot Ciara had just washed. "An Irish woman was living on the island over one hundred years ago and she saw how the women were making fishing nets and how poor they were. She believed if they could make nets they could make lace, and she taught them how to do it." I took the platter of mixed cheeses and meats from Ciara and placed it on the set table before going back for the bowl of pasta. "The lace then became world famous. They made a dress for Sophia Loren and some other famous people. I bet there will be a four-leaf shamrock somewhere in the dress's design if you look closely."

"I'll check for sure. I do hope the dress is still there. Perhaps you can come with me tomorrow to see? It would be so nice to have a second option and a woman's opinion at that."

Ciara picked up a small brass bell from the side table and gave it a shake. The tinkle brought the guys to the room. Paolo had showered, and Valentino had had a nap.

"It works wonders and saves my vocal cords," Ciara smiled, referring to the bell while taking her seat at the table. "We'll make up two plates and put it aside for your friends. What time should they arrive at?"

"You know one is a dog?"

"Yes, but she still needs to eat and can still be counted as a friend. They are friends in permanent onesies, I say."

What a perfect description and from an 80-year-old who knew what a onesie was.

"I think it will be another hour before they get here. Taking parking into account and all."

"Valentino, have you heard that Anna has been arrested for the murder?" Ciara said, casually, as she passed the pasta.

Paolo caught his breath so quickly it caused a crumb to go down the wrong tube and had him coughing for at least a minute before he could clarify, "Aunt Ciara, you cannot say that! She has not been arrested, she has been taken in to the station to be asked some questions."

"Same thing." She tutted.

"No, it's not! Questioning people who knew her is perfectly routine. Being arrested for murder is a very different thing."

"Anyway, I think Daisy is right. I think Paolo has got himself the wrong woman."

"What?" Paolo exclaimed. His aunt was getting out of line with her off-the-cuff remarks.

"I mean Anna. I don't think she did the murder I think you have got yourself the wrong woman."

"Ohhh..." Paolo sat back in his chair, relieved he didn't have to make a choice between his aunt and I. Although I felt smugly confident I would win if it came to it.

"Valentino, Daisy was saying how the corpse was in an artistic pose like a classical painting," she continued on with her roll of obscurities.

"That's not quite-" I interrupted her bluntness.

"Actually, now that you say that Daisy..." Valentino said, talking over me while mopping his lips with a napkin. "The pose she was in, was quite like a photo I saw of painting believed to be by Klimt... The Woman with Pearls. Daisy is also a big fan of Klimt," he casually threw in.

"I don't know that one. Which art museum is it in?" Glad to be away from the subject of the murder, I went on to explain to Ciara, "If I'm in a city and there is a Klimt painting in the art museum, then it's my first stop on the tourist path."

"Unfortunately, it went missing around the time of the Nazi heist. We believe it was in the castle fire in Austria with his other works. Although this particular piece had not been verified as his at that point. It had just been found in an attic somewhere and was in the process of being assessed."

"I always wondered how they assess paintings. That Russian woman at the party, Natasha, explained it a little," I said.

"A work of art goes through several processes. For instance, we have an X-ray machine at the restoration studios that can see through the paint onto the initial markings on the canvas. And then, of course, there are the materials used such as the paints, thinners, canvas, any that were done after-"

"The atomic bombs, they have two different isotopes."

"Ah yes, you know this already." Ciara passed me the olive oil and balsamic vinegar duo of her 1920s art nouveau bottle set for my salad.

"That's how Raphael discovered the Vase of Flowers was a forgery, wasn't it?" said Paolo.

"Yes, that's right. Do you know what he ever did with that painting?" Valentino looked at Ciara.

"He probably has it hanging in his bathroom," smirked Ciara. "Or he put his foot through it. I think he was banking on it bringing him fame and fortune."

Paolo sat back in his chair, looking at the wisteria dance in the breeze. "Do you think perhaps it could have been one of the students who may have been trying to forge the painting by Klimt and pass it off to an unsuspecting art dealer. Or perhaps that chap Filippo..."

"I think Filippo is beyond forging paintings. He is an excellent artist in his own right and has had exhibitions all over the world. He is also one of the best art restorers in the world, so not short of money," said Ciara.

"And he's not the type capable of murder," said Paolo.

"Where have I heard that before?" I smirked.

"And he's not a potter. Besides, you saw his reaction today. That wasn't an act. He went over and threw up in the corner of the room after you left."

"But then who? And what would have been the reason to kill her?" I wondered.

"Jealousy," chimed in Valentino. "She was a beautiful woman with a lot of admirers. Jealousy can make a person do terrible things," he continued, bringing out a bottle of wine to the table.

"Personally, I think it has to do with deception. I think a student was trying to create a forgery," Ciara insisted. "Find the painting that was being done and it will tell the story. My mother used to always tell me that each painting has a story behind it and a message to tell."

"Like every great man has an even greater woman behind him." Valentino winked at her.

"One of those students' portfolios could have the back story you are looking for. Have a look through them. You might find the clues that you are looking for," she continued. "These student restorers are being trained to mimic the great artists' work. They are being taught by the best. Any of them could paint a perfect reproduction and then sell it as the genuine article. Especially if it is a relatively unknown Klimt."

"But with the test now of the isobars or whatever you call them, then they would never get away with it," Paolo said, helping himself to seconds of the pasta.

"They might on the black market," said Ciara. "A lot of very shady art deals go on. They could sell it to an unsuspecting collector that has no notion of isotopes. In my view, you're looking for a skilled painter. The girl probably wanted a cut of the proceeds from the sale, and would have promised to blackmail him if he didn't comply with her request. He killed her in a fashion to say that she needed to be silenced," she said matter-of-factly.

"You should have been the one that is an agent, Aunt Ciara," laughed Paolo.

No one seemed to notice his slip up but me. I had just found him out. But then we were all distracted by the excited yelp of a large dog coming up the external stairs. "It's them, they're here. Sophia and my friend in a permanent onesie–Shadow."

14

I needed a shower after the amount of slobbery kisses Shadow heaped upon my face. I freshened up while Sophia and Shadow had dinner. Sophia and I then took our hairy house mate on a long walk down by the Arno while we caught up. Paolo knew he was not wanted, so went to visit a friend of his to give his aunt and Valentino some alone time together. I knew he hoped that if they had time to step out of the whirlwind of events, they might change their minds about getting married.

"Seriously?" asked Sophia, as we strolled along the pathway beside the setting sun's mandarin-toned shimmers on the Arno. "I was wondering why you were so tense and uptight. I can't believe another dead body, and both when you have been with Paolo. If he wasn't such a nice guy, I would think he was hexed."

"I know it's just one of those awful coincidences that you only read about in mystery books. We are still having fun together, but I think he's hiding something from me." I took a deep breath. I had to spit out the inkling that sat in my stomach, eating up my insides if I didn't release it to someone.

"I think he is working for the police, still undercover. He let something slip at dinner about being an agent and they include him too much in the investigations for an ex-cop..." Verbalising the thought instantly made me feel lighter. It was this that had me wound up like a tight spring.

"Have you asked him?" Sophia was always good at stating the obvious solutions.

"Sort of, but he said it was not a conversation for now..."

"Well, ask him again."

"I will whenever the right time for discussing such a thing comes up... Anyway, let's get back to talking about the wedding and what has to be done." I said, suddenly feeling like I didn't want to discuss it anymore.

"I'm all ears. What do you need me to do?"

"How about you handle the fluffy side of things and I'll deal with the logistics." This didn't really need to be said, as logistics were always my strength, while Sophia excelled at fluffiness.

"I've been trying to get a hold of the restaurant but they never answer the phone so we can call in on our way back, it's close to the apartment." Shadow let a 'Please,' groan. I guessed there must have been a gelato bar within sniffing distance. "Alright, since we are on vacation."

Just as we turned the corner, the mint green and red facade of Gino's Gelateria was before us. Shadow yelped and gave a little skip in the air.

"A cup with chocolate orange and pistachio for me. Rum and butter and English trifle in a cone for my friend and a honey gelato cup for the pup." I'd order favourite gelato treats so often in our hometown of Trasimeno that I forgot including the dog in our order raised eyebrows in places that weren't familiar with us.

We found shade in a quiet spot under a candy cane striped umbrella outside the shop and as we slurped our way through the deliciousness, I continued with the completed 'to-do's' on the list.

"I've already put in a call to the PR company about media timing of the big reveal, and the Lord Mayor is dealing directly with Valentino and Ciara about the necessary paperwork. Have you had any success with a photographer and heard from Davide yet?"

"I've put in requests to four photographers, all are booked up." I automatically bent forward and wiped some dripping ice-cream from her chin with a napkin. "I've another two possibilities, including the guy we met in Rome. He seemed alright, didn't he?"

"Yes, his photos were lovely, you'd never know there was a murder investigation going on in the background, so he's just the type of photographer we need for this wedding. Maybe he can have it as his byline, 'Beautiful Wedding Photos with no murder evidence showing'."

We were still laughing about it by the time we had left the gelateria and had crossed the street. The Ponte Vecchio was now behind us and the majestic grey pillars of the Uffizi entrance ahead of us. "According to my phone," I said, stopping for a moment and swivelling slightly to line myself up with the red dotted directions on my screen to the restaurant. "It's just down here on the left."

Sophia continued through her 'To do list' that I had given her earlier.

"Davide is on board, although he nearly had a blue monkey when I told him who it was for. He kept and saying he couldn't possibly do another vase of flowers in such a brief space of time. I have no idea what he was talking about but I told him not to worry, it is just a bride's bouquet and some boutonnieres, there's no decoration needed."

"Here it is." I said, looking up from my screen. "It has a pretty front that is a good start." The teal arched doors with geometric shaped glass cut outs and warm glowing lanterns on either side of the doorway had attracted a good crowd inside. "This isn't a good sign. I bet it's booked up for Thursday."

Once inside, we both immediately scanned the room with our wedding eyes. The wooden beams begged the question of how high a ladder we'd need to drape string lighting. The width of the tables had us counting multiples on our fingers behind our backs of how many could fit in the room with the tables long or spaced apart. The scent of the place, the air flow, the instant atmosphere, any eyesores we needed to disguise with a well-placed plant or flower urn. The crockery, the linens, the chairs. All of this was absorbed within the first eight seconds of walking in the door of any venue when doing a site inspection.

Glasses were clinking, plates were being emptied, waiters were smiling. It all looked positive except for one thing. The head-waiter was walking towards us shaking his head. If Shadow wasn't going to be allowed in, I didn't want the wedding to happen here.

15

"**G**ood evening ladies, I am afraid we are full this evening." He said, patting Shadow on the head.

"Oh, we are not interested in eating here..." I said, nearly laughing in his face with relief that he liked Shadow. "Well, we are... but just not tonight. We are interested in Thursday?"

"I am sorry we close on Thursdays." He looked like he was going to cry for us with disappointment.

"That's a relief!" I said, slapping my hands together.

"I am sorry?" The shiny headed man looked at me, confused.

"Valentino and Ciara, you know them?"

"Of course, they are my favourite and most loyal customers."

"They are getting married on Thursday and they specifically asked to have their wedding reception here for about 20 friends."

"Oh DIO!" His voice screeched high enough for the surrounding tables to look to see if he had caught something in his zipper. "They are getting married?" His hands were on his mouth, stopping him from screeching in delight.

"Of course I will open especially for them. It would be an honour and how exciting! What time would they like?"

"Dinner at 7pm?... but we would like access from about 12 noon."

"Of course! Anything for them, but why so early?"

"We've a little decorating to do–if you don't mind–but don't worry, your place will be back to its old self the following morning."

"Okay, if that is what they want. I will ask Julia to be here at 12 to let you in. She is my daughter and head chef. She will help you find whatever you need."

"Great, we need all the help we can get to make this happen at such short notice. Here's my card. Could you email me the menu choices?"

"I can, but I can nearly tell you 100 percent already what they will choose. It will be the truffled egg as a starter, cinghiale tagliatelle as the first plate and Florentine-style steak, infused with rosemary and sage as the main course. Give me your card and I will send you a perfect menu for them with one or two alternatives for each plate. But I can bet you one of my best wines they will go with the first choice. All you need to do is confirm the number of guests with me tomorrow. Here please take my card as well."

From his inside pocket, he handed me his business card with a small sketch of the front of his restaurant on it. "See you Thursday," he called after us as we left.

"This is turning out to be one of our fastest and easiest weddings ever, even with a murder thrown into the mix," I said to Sophia.

Back on the street where the ancient doors to Ciara's apartment were, the lights glowed from the small puddles between the cobbles left by the earlier sudden downpour. Florence had quickly recovered from the rain invasion and now the night was warm and balmy.

"Careful!" Sophia shouted, pushing me against the wall. Shadow leapt in front of me, taking the hit from a puddle being sprayed up against us by a car going well over the 20 mph permitted on the side street. But it was still slow enough for me to see the concerned face of the driver. He looked like death warmed up and his eyes as big and as round as those in a stuffed teddy bear. He didn't see us.

"That was Raphael."

"Who is Raphael?"

"The guy who is engaged to the dead girl's friend, Anna. He must be going in to pick her up from the station... Maybe she is being charged with it, he looked worried."

We were buzzed in through the gate and Shadow was already leading the way across the courtyard, proud to know where she was going. Half-way up the external stone steps, I heard her bark. "That's not a 'let me in' bark, that's an excited I found something bark," Sophia observed.

"You are getting to know her as well as I do!"

Sure enough, a rectangular flat package about two feet by three feet long, wrapped in brown paper and string, sat outside the door of Ciara's apartment with an envelope attached. Just as we lifted it, Valentino opened the door. "What's that you have, are you bringing us gifts now?" he chuckled.

"It's not from me I'm afraid, it was just sitting out here, but it is for you and Ciara."

As with all polite people, Ciara carefully opened the envelop first. Unlike me, who cannot wait and rips open a present as soon as it is in my hands before looking at the card.

Dear Ciara and Valentino,

I have heard about the Vase of Flowers being returned on Thursday. I have also heard that you're getting married on that day, too. I think it is appro-

priate you have this as a wedding gift. It may not be the original, but after Thursday, you may agree that what you now have is an improvement.

After the shocking day we all have had, I am going to the Czech Republic with Anna as she wants to help make funeral arrangements for her friend and be with Julia's family as they were close growing up. I am heartbroken for Anna. I never thought she could be so sad.

So I will not be here for your wedding. But when you look at this, think of me always–

Raphael the great artist.

X

Raphael

Valentino untied the string and folded the paper back. It was a canvas. The fake version of the Vase of Flowers.

"Wow, that is beautiful," said Sophia. "Look at the detail in the butterfly wings. Did the guy we just saw going off in the car paint this?"

"No, no, no, he would be in proper trouble if he did. He found it in a flea market in France and thought it was the real thing, although he denies he thought it was the original, but everyone else fell for it," said Valentino, looking at the painting with pure disgust.

"I would have been sure that he did the painting himself, except he showed no interest in claiming the finder's reward when it was offered to him. And he could do with the money, I think. His apartment is worth, a lot but his work down at the studios is more administrative than specialised. He's not paid much," added Ciara as both she and Valentino stared at the painting. "Why does he think we would like this? Someone trying to dupe us into believing our favourite painting had been found?"

"Well, we can't burn it, which I would like to do–"

"Burn it?" Sophia looked horrified at Valentino's suggestion. He was too focused on a solution to hear her "Nor can we give it away. He would be massively offended. What should we do with it?"

"I'm not too sure... how about we put it into the guest room where Paolo and Daisy are staying and get rid of that hideous Ugly Child painting. It will save Paolo having to dump it after I die," Ciara said, returning from the hallway cupboard with a towel for Shadow.

"Good idea. I'll leave a bottle of wine outside his door as a thank you."

"I'm sorry we ever spotted it walking by his place that day." Ciara gave Shadow a rub with the towel, drying off the puddle water. "I couldn't resist having a peek in as it's the only time I ever saw his door wide open. I think we are still the only ones who have ever seen inside that apartment."

"It's probably because it's a chaotic mess, everything in it was covered with dust sheets. It was like he was hiding bodies our something. And candles lighting everywhere. Is he trying to save on electricity do you think?"

Ciara pushed the painting aside on the table. "Paolo, be a dear and take the painting to your room the next time you are going that way... Now who wants a cocktail?"

16

S he's there again. The girl, about 13 years old, pale faced, ruddy cheeks, her long black hair kept from her face with a satin bow, white high neck white dress. She's behind the attic door. Banging. She wants to get out and only I can hear her. This time I hear what she says, but it makes no sense to me. It sounds German.

I woke in a sweat, glued to the bed. Paralysed for a moment, staring up at the attic. The lock was gone. I lay waiting for it to open at any moment and for her to appear or to bang again. The banging started again, but it was from the street below where a worker was putting a new sign over the handmade paper shop, not from the attic.

"Are you okay? You were making whimpering sounds in your sleep?" Paolo put his arm around me and tried to pull me closer, but my body was still rigid. "I had a bad dream. There was a girl in the attic trying to get out." Vocalising it helped separate the dream from reality and my body softened. Paolo turned over on his other side "It's too early, I'll let her out later."

The constant joker was soon back to sleep, but his soft snoring was not enough to drown out the adrenaline pulsating in my ears. The

Ugly Child on the wall with the weird eyes was staring at me. She had to go if I was to sleep in this room another night. Creeped out, there was no rescuing my sleep. It was time for some tea.

"You're up early. The kettle has just boiled. Would you like some tea with milk?" Ciara was up first again as always and took great joy asking me every time she offered me a cup of tea if I still wanted milk in it. She found the idea highly amusing.

"Yes please, I'll make it though. You stay where you are." But she was already on her feet and we were both walking into the kitchen. "I have an appointment with the dress shop at 10am. You will come a long with me, won't you? Just to have a second opinion, I don't want to be mutton dressed as lamb... Are you okay, Daisy? You look like you've seen a ghost."

"I'll be fine after I've had some tea. I just had a nightmare, that's all. I think the attic door is freaking me out a little. I dreamt there was a young girl locked up there trying to get out. She said-"

Ciara dropped the tea bag on the floor instead of my cup. "Did she have long black hair and a Victorian white dress?"

My wide eyes gave her the answer. "I've dreamt of her too. That is why I got the lock put on the attic some years ago. I don't believe in ghosts, but the dream was too real. It spooked me and-"

"Ciara, the lock is gone." I said, my voice trembling.

Ciara laughed out loud, "Oh don't worry, the ghost didn't take it. Clive brought over his ladder yesterday evening, when you were all out. Your friend, the florist, was there visiting him. The chap in the purple suit?"

"Davide?"

"Yes, anyway, Valentino looked into the attic yesterday evening to check the noises, but he couldn't see anything. I'll get Paolo-"

"What are you both planning for me now?" We both jumped with the suddenness of Paolo being in the room without hearing him come in.

"You gave us both a fright," laughed Ciara. "I need you to put the lock back on the attic. Valentino had a look into it yesterday evening, but couldn't see anything."

"Why didn't you wait until I got back?" said Paolo. "Valentino shouldn't be climbing at his age."

"He wanted to do it. Don't worry, there's a lot we do that people think at our age we shouldn't be doing." She winked as she took her tea with lemon, not milk, over to the kitchen island and made herself comfortable on a high stool.

I leaned my back against the counter beside the coffee machine.

Paolo and my eyebrows raised in mutual surprise at his aunt's last jibe. Paolo didn't give it any space to develop.

"Is Valentino up yet?" he asked. "The station just texted me. They want him to go down there this morning. They have a few questions."

"Oh dear, I hope all this horribleness will not interfere with the wedding or honeymoon. He's in the shower I will go and get him."

"It's just procedure, don't worry, I'll tell them he'll be busy on Thursday," smiled Paolo, kissing his aunt on the forehead before she eased up out of her chair and went to get Valentino. "And a honeymoon? Where are you going?" he called after her, but she was already out of earshot.

Paolo stuck a cup under the espresso machine and pressed the button. "I'll bring him down to the station and try to speed them up. They probably just want to get the register of who had access to the studios at the weekend. I'm surprised they haven't requested it already."

"Well, it's only the start of day three of the investigation, I suppose."

"That's a long time. If I was the murderer I would have left the country by now."

Shadow was up on her feet and out of her bed, which had been moved to the hallway after her saving me from the puddle soaking. "I'll take her for a walk around outside. You go have your shower, I know you have a busy day ahead." He knew me too well.

"Thanks, that is very considerate of you Paolo Ferrari." I kissed him on the cheek playfully as he walked down the hallway with his espresso cup in hand and an excited Shadow by his leg.

I stood at the front door and watch them walk around the walkway, past Raphael's door with the bottle of wine outside and down towards Clive's apartment. They walked in unison and for a moment I let the word 'love' play on my lips before getting to grips with myself.

Back inside, Sophia was up and looking fresh and ready for action, which was unusual for her night owl self. Ciara was fussing around Valentino, who was grabbing his hat and looking for his car keys that were already in his hand, "Oh Paolo said he'd take you to the station, he's just taken Shadow for a quick walk."

"It is alright, I'll go by myself. I'm a big boy, I can handle it. I'll be back soon." He gave Ciara a quick kiss, dipped his hat at Sophia and I and he was out the door before I had taken another sip of my tea.

"Are you not ready to go yet, I don't want to be late," said a perfectly groomed Ciara.

"Gosh, I seem to be running behind everyone else today. I'm sorry hmm, is it okay if Sophia goes dress shopping with you instead? She's much better than me at that sort of thing?"

"Of course, just as long as it is not Valentino, I don't mind who comes."

"Did someone say dress shopping? I'm your girl. Do we need to take the car?"

"No, no, it is just across the bridge, a lovely walk at this time in the morning. I do hope the dress is still there and looks good on me. If not, I can always wear the white pantsuit that I wore on my birthday."

"You will not! You're to come back with something new to wear on your wedding day."

"That pantsuit is Gucci I'll have you know."

"It doesn't matter; you are to buy something new. We can't be looking back on photos in years to come and trying to figure out if they were from your birthday or wedding. You need different outfits to differentiate the days," I said.

"Valentino and I don't plan to be having children anytime soon. So there will be no future generations to confuse with photos. And that's another thing, we don't need a photographer for the wedding, just a few snaps on people's phones is enough." Her dimples were showing again. "I'll just get my bag and we'll be off."

"Sophia," I said, as we were waiting for Ciara to come back. "Do you know what 'das gemalde' means?" I guessed it was German and knew that was one of the five or six languages she spoke fluently.

"It's German for 'the painting-'"

"And 'finde mich'? I'm guessing is 'find me'?"

"Yes, why?" Sophia bit into an apple just as Ciara arrived back.

"Are you ready to go, young lady?"

"I sure am." Sophia linked Ciara's arm, and they both went out the front door chattering away like school girls.

I didn't have time to answer Sophia's question with; "it is what the ghost in the attic said to me."

17

While in the shower, I heard a bang outside the bathroom door. I knew I was the only one in the house. So I stayed there. Arms frozen mid soaping, taking shallow breaths just enough to keep my heart thumping, wishing Shadow and Paolo to be back. My wish instantly came true as I heard Shadow's excited bark outside while Paolo fiddled with the key in the front door lock.

Shower turned off, dressing gown slipped on. I cautiously eased open the bedroom door. But there was something jamming it from opening or was it someone holding it closed? Just as that thought hit and panic welled up in my throat, I heard Shadow's nails skidding on the parquet flooring as she took a speedy sharp right into our bedroom from the hall. Knowing that she would have had a vicious bark rather than her excited where-are-you-hiding-I-want-to-show-you-something yelp, gave me the confidence to push the door a little harder and the blockage moved. Looking down behind the door, I could see it was the Ugly Child painting that had fallen off the wall and was now jammed on the floor at an angle between the door and wall.

Paolo bounced into the room after his new best four-legged pal. "We walked past a Doggy Beauty Parlour on the way back and they gave Shadow a quick bubble bath and blow dry."

Shadow did an excited twirl, chasing her tail, showing off her new shiny do.

"You look beautiful, girl! All the stinky puddle water is gone. You are all set for the wedding."

"I passed by my aunt with Sophia. I've never seen my aunt look so happy." He was zipping me up in the linen shift dress I had just slipped on. I noticed in the long mirror I was facing, that his expression was tight facial muscles rather than relaxed and happy about what he just said. "Then what's the face for, do you still not like Valentino?"

"That's the thing, I do really like him now. I can see he is truly in love with her and she obviously with him. They deserve to do whatever makes them happy... but I just called the station and the police are not just asking him general questions about the students, they are questioning him as a suspect..."

"As a suspect?... Valentino?" I said, spitting the words out, nearly laughing. "He couldn't have done it, he's way too sweet. What has given them that idea?"

"It was Anna... she said he had an affair with Julia and his motive would have been Julia threatening to tell Ciara after she heard they got engaged on Saturday."

"Seriously? He was having an affair?" My chin was nearly on the ground.

"I know. I am finding it difficult to believe too. But murdering someone to silence them is a strong motive. If it's true, I'll kill him myself for breaking my aunt's heart."

"I'm sure it's not true. Wasn't Filippo her partner? In all fairness, Valentino is a good-looking man, but he is nearly 80 compared to Filippo, who is well-built and good looking. If I were investigating this case, I would consider Filippo as a suspect more so than Valentino if the affair story was true.

"Killing his girlfriend having found out she is sleeping with an old dear when he could fulfil her needs, if you get what I mean. Pride more so than jealousy fuelled." I shook my hair from the towel and gave it a quick brush before squeezing some mousse in it and leaving it to dry naturally. I could see Paolo twitch uneasily when he realised I was not going to use the hair dryer on the dressing table. He had the ingrained Italian fear of wet hair leading to a multitude of ailments. Even Ciara couldn't wait to dry off Shadow the evening before.

"That's a good point," he said, hanging my damp towel on the towel rack in the ensuite. "Actually, I may call Emanuele and point that out to him. They seemed to be quick with their questioning of Filippo. I think they should bring him in again and go deeper. Perhaps Anna is trying to deflect the blame from Filippo. Him and Raphael seem to be good friends. I can't imagine Valentino having an affair... I'm sure it will be all cleared up soon and he will be sent home."

I wasn't really listening to him. Something in the corner of my eye was distracting me. "Shadow, what on earth are you doing?" She had the jammed painting cornered behind the ensuite door and was licking the Ugly Child's face like it was an open wound on her paw.

"Why is the painting on the floor?" asked Paolo, noticing it for the first time

"It fell off when I was in the shower. You both came in just after it happened so I haven't had a chance yet to put it back up."

"No problem, I'll do it." Paolo went over and lifted the painting up to where it was previously hanging, but stopped. "That's weird. The old nail seems to have fallen out of the wall, it's probably only been there 50 years," he jested.

"Honestly, you have to get that painting out of this room. It just gives me the creeps and I am sure it caused the nightmare I had last night. Do as your aunt asked and hang up the Vase of Flowers instead and get rid of that one."

"I can't throw the painting out, no matter how much she hates it. My grandmother painted it and I'm sentimental about these things. I'll put it in the attic. With all the fuss about the wedding, she'll forget about it and just presume I threw it out. I saw the ladder in the hallway coming in. I'll go get it."

While Paolo struggled to straighten the ladder and put it in place at the hatch door. I went and fetched the Vase of Flowers painting from the sitting room.

"I might take some of my mother's painting equipment home. This trip has made me think about painting again," Paolo said as he pushed open the hatch and hoisted himself into the black hole, his phone torch beaming from where he had it braced in his mouth. "Hand me up the painting." He leaned down and took the painting from me, which I'd retrieved from Shadow's tongue again.

"Honestly Shadow, what on earth? Look at your tongue now, it's all white."

As I stuck the fifty-year-old nail back into the hole where it fell from, I could hear Paolo rummaging around in the attic, I was imagining the complimentary spiders that would come attached to the old painting gear that Paolo intended to take back in my precious Mabel Carr.

The nail was a bit wobbly, but it was solid enough to hang the Vase of Flowers from.

"What the hell!" shouted Paolo, distracting me from trying to straighten the painting.

"What's the matter?" I called up.

"Daisy, go and get me a jiffy bag out of the kitchen, a big one."

I knew what he was talking about. The caterers had left a pile of them on top of the fridge.

"What do you need that for?" I called up again, louder.

"Just go and get it." It was the first time he had ever been abrupt with me. I wasn't happy about it but gave him the benefit of the doubt that there may be a good reason.... And there was.

In the jiffy bag dangling from his hand, as he made his way down the ladder, was a coiled potter's wire. On each end of the wire were two thick wooden dowels. Two thick wooden, blood splattered dowels.

"I think I have just found the murder weapon."

18

"Poor Aunt Ciara. She will be broken-hearted," said Paolo, sitting staring at the jiffy-bagged weapon he's thrown onto the middle of the dining room table. I got us glasses of sparkling water and joined him. We needed to step out of the tornado for a moment to get our heads around what was happening.

"I just can't believe he is such a completely different person than the one we have both met. I can't imagine such a sweet man cheating on your aunt and now being a murderer? Are we both that bad at reading people's character?"

"It's always the ones you least expect... the nice ones."

"But you're sweet and nice?"

"Yes, but like you, I am exceptional. That's why we are an excellent match." He was so Italian, always managing a compliment or chat up line, even when dealing with a murder.

"Hey, don't get distracted we are not match-making here... Are we sure it's him? I mean Sweet Valentino that opens the window and whooshes flies out rather than killing them?" I knew Paolo had also seen Valentino do this the day before. A wasp had flown in and landed on some leftover cake. Ciara shouted at him to kill it, but instead he guided it out the window with the comment "All God's creatures are entitled to life."

"Yes, but he is an Italian man with passion too and how else would it have got there?... Ciara said he had been up in the attic only yesterday. Before that it was locked... Unless... you did it and put it up there?"

"Or you..." I answered, both of us held each other's eye contact waiting for the other to blink.

"I can't believe we are doing this. Honestly, it's no time for games," I said, breaking the starring contest. "What are we going to do?"

"I'll have to bring it to the station immediately. Poor Aunt Ciara. I feel like killing him myself. How am I going to break this news to her?" Paolo rested his face against his steepled hands.

I put my arm on his bicep and gave it a squeeze, expecting the tender touch to give him comfort, but instead the hardness of it just gave me a wooshy feeling in my stomach.

"When Sophia and your aunt get back, I'll keep Ciara here so you can tell her when you return. It will be better for her to hear the news in her own surroundings rather than at a police station."

"Perhaps while I'm out, you can tell her?" his eyes were pleading.

The helium filled floating heart shaped balloon in my stomach suddenly turned to toxic lead. "I really can't believe you..."

His bottom lip stuck out, and he sat back in his chair as if my blast of vehemence was so strong that it pushed him back. If he was looking for an explanation, he was going to get one.

"You duped me into coming to Florence on the pretence of a romantic weekend away and so far, in three days, I've had to endure your 80-year-old Aunt's birthday–although, I have to admit, that was fun–find a dead body, be questioned about the said dead body, plan a speedy wedding, put up with your moodiness about your aunt's engagement and now you want me to be the one to tell this woman who I have met three days ago that the man she is about to marry is a murderer?"

"You must really love me to put up with so much." He was chewing a candy he had plucked from the bonbon dish near the jiffy bag.

"Love?" I looked at him, horrified. "You don't know how close I am to packing up and going back to Trasimeno to my vegetable patch."

His eyes held mine as he took a sip of water and gave me big blood hound 'please pet me' eyes over the glass rim. "Have I been moody?... If so, I am sorry."

A large exhale of air shot through my nostrils like a pressurised gas cylinder's tap being opened. With the air went the buildup of tension and stress. That's all it took, an apology and an acknowledgement. And those eyes.

"Would you really prefer to spend time with your cucumbers than be here with me?"

He reached across the table and took my hand, rubbing the back of it with his thumb. I was trying not to laugh.

"But come on, you thrive in these types of situations. You'd much rather be here, amongst the chaos rather than tending to your cucumbers." He had a point. While the idea of being retired from wedding planning in a year's time seemed attractive, I sometimes woke up in a cold sweat wondering what the hell I was going to do with myself all day. But I wasn't going to tell him that.

"I am the same, we are like... due gocce d'acqua."

"Two drops of water?... Do you mean two peas in a pod?"

"Yes, we say that too in Italy, but we also say like two drops of water. I prefer this one for us somehow, it is... cooler."

I felt far from cool. My mind had gone somewhere else. The stress and tension that had momentarily lapsed was replaced with worry and concern. "Gosh, I hope they give her the money back on the dress she'll never get to wear."

"I think that will be the last of her worries." Paolo got up from the table and reluctantly bagged the jiffy bag into his knapsack.

"Here, take Mabel Carr rather than walking," I said, handing him the keys off the coat stand in the hallway. Shadow came out to the door to tail wag Paolo goodbye, and I went in and did my nervous Irish habit thing of putting on the kettle even though it was climbing to 30 degrees outside. A cup of tea can solve everything.

Just as the kettle climaxed, the doorbell made me jerk. Sophia bundled in through the door with four large bags. "Hi, I'm back. The dress is just gorgeous, and she bought you a present too. She is such a sweet, sweet woman."

I looked out the door behind her. "Where's Aunt Ciara?"

"Oh Valentino, texted her. He forgot his wallet, so she has gone to pick him up from the station. She just grabbed a taxi outside to go get him."

"I don't think he'll be coming back," I muttered, closing the door after her.

"What do you mean?" I was surprised she heard me. I usually can get away with lots of under breath mutterings around Sophia because of her not one hundred percent hearing.

I sighed. "Let's have a cup of tea. I've something to tell you."

19

Sophia sat staring into the bottom of her cup as if trying to read fortunes from the tea leaves. "But he's so nice... and gentle." She was taking his murdering ways to heart.

"Well, who else could have put it in the attic?" I said, putting on my practical and logical head, removing the emotions that had built up previously.

"Oh My God..." she said, dropping her teaspoon on to the saucer. "Could it have been Aunt Ciara?"

"What? Has the heat gone to your head? You just said the little old lady was sweet? "

"Yes, but she is also passionate and strong. I mean, there was no problem with her walking fast to the shop. I had to hurry to keep up."

My mouth was still gaping open at her even considering Ciara as a suspect. "Sophia! She doesn't even have a manly mug in the house... only these wafer-thin vintage china cups that I am afraid to drink out of in case they break. She's had them forever. Surely if she was the murdering type, a few would have been smashed against the wall by this point or at least a handle or two broken off in a rage?" My argument was random, I agree, but Sophia's suggestion was so obscure, my randomness was a good match.

"No, hear me out," said Sophia, piecing together a puzzle with Ciara the murderous octogenarian as the central image. "Ciara insisted on carrying the heavier bags. She said it was good for bone strength. And she told me a thing or too that made my ears burn, there's no lack of passion in their relationship, let me tell you. That's why she never had Julia over to the house... because Julia and Valentino had a thing going on for a while when Julia first came to Italy... before Ciara and Valentino started seeing each other."

"She knew about Valentino's and Julia's affair?"

"Well, she knew they were together previous to her. But it was long finished. Julia was in a steady relationship with that guy called Filippo."

"So you think the relationship between Julia and Valentino started again or that Julia still had the hots for him and Ciara killed her as a crime of passion or jealousy for previously having her man?"

Sophia thought for a moment. "Nah, on second thoughts scrap the idea."

I have to admit; I entertained the thought of Aunt Ciara being a murderous villain for a moment. But then I remembered how exhausted Ciara was after her party. There was no way she would have got up in the middle of the night and gone to kill someone. For that matter, neither would Valentino. He did get up several times a night, like most elderly men, and he was prone to early morning walks but to go and kill Julia just to tidy things up relationship wise before his wedding seemed a bit far-fetched.

My thoughts were interrupted by a rapping on the front door.

"Who could that be? How did they get past the gate?" I froze. All this talk of possibly living with the enemy had made me jittery.

Sophia just shrugged. "I'm in a complete stranger's house. How the hell would I know?"

"Hide the bags quick! It's probably Ciara having forgotten her keys and if we have to break this news to her, I think it's best if her wedding dress is out of sight. She'll be heart-broken enough."

"Where will I hide them?" Sophia jumped to her feet.

"I don't know. Find a place. QUICK!" I said urgently while making my way to the hallway. "Who is it?" I called through the door.

"It's me, Davide."

I look through the peephole and sure enough, there was Davide in a powder blue suit staring back in at me with his tongue sticking out, knowing I would look through the peephole.

"Surprise! It's me and I brought wine," he said, wafting in without waiting for an invitation as soon as I opened the door.

"Is that the wine that was left outside the door across the way?" I knew it was.

"You found me out! But we might as well drink it anyway as it's been there for days." He was exaggerating again. "Don't close the door, Clive is coming." Davide leaned the top half of his body back out the door. "Come on Amore," he called.

"Amore?" I stood holding the door.

Davide winked at me with a big grin splashed across his face. "Yes, you and I have a lot of catching up to do," he whispered, swishing past me, followed by quiet Clive with a coy smile, who shook my hand formally before following Davide. Clive had small twinkly eyes framed with long eyelashes. He was the same height as me but deceptively looked taller, probably because he was more stocky.

"Have you seen the plastic ivy on the beams of that restaurant? It has to go before the wedding, so we are here to pick up Clive's ladder...

You are having tea? Great, let's have tea first, then we'll get the ladder." Davide's melodic TV-presenter-style voice had filled the apartment with love and lightness again.

"Davide... something has come up... there might not be a wedding."

"Whaaaat? Oh, Daisy! You know these pre wedding jitters, they always get over them. I haven't asked the restaurant if I can remove the offending ivy but I'm going to anyway. They can then at least wash the dust off it. I'll be doing them a favour. And then we'll be ready for the wedding with or without jitters."

I gave a weak smile. It wasn't my place to tell the biggest gossip in Italy that sweet Valentino was going to be done for murder.

"Actually, Sophia and I just finished tea, so let's get the ladder and have tea afterwards." We walked into the bedroom where the ladder was still in place and the hatch was still open. "Clive, would you be so kind and close the hatch before you take the ladder away?" I asked, trying to sound like a helpless damsel in distress. "Noises are coming from that attic and it gives me the heebie-jeebies at night."

"You are hearing noises because the attics are all interconnected, there are no dividing walls. So if I'm up in my attic or any of the other residents bang on the water pipes in their apartments or are shifting anything around in their attic space, you'll hear it here. Come up and have a look." Clive squeezed his well-rounded podgy body into the dark hole as if being sucked up a shoot like Augustus Gloop in Charlie and the Chocolate Factory.

With Clive up there, I felt it a good time to go up and check if there just happened to be a girl in a white dress wandering around a little lost–just in case anyone was missing a Victorian child.

I peeped my head and shoulders cautiously through. Dust caught in invisible tubes of golden light danced from the round air holes in the side walls down onto the floor like wide light sabers. Together with a skylight at the far end of the building's roof, there was enough visibility to see the items stored near to the hatch hole.

Other than the Ugly Child painting Paolo had thrown up there earlier, there were piles of crockery and silver domes dulled by dust and years. Across from heaped dishes there was a clear patch of angular shapes with less dust on the wooden boards, where something had been recently cleared. Something was missing.

"The attic to my apartment is way over there." Clive pointed into the darkness. "So you see there is nothing to be scared of."

"What about over there?" I point to a shaft of light coming up from below on the opposite side of the building. "I don't know... that is strange, though. They seemed to have left their attic open. I'll go have a look."

20

With the light from the torch on his phone, Clive made it over to the other side of the wide-open attic space.

"It must be Raphael's," Clive called back as he got to the open hatch at the other side of the vast, dark space. I could see his face lit by the weak light coming up from below the open hatch. "This must be his studio room as there is painting stuff all over it... Raphael?" He called down, waiting for a response below.

"He's not there," I called over. "He's away for a few days."

"Ah okay. Hmmm. There's a cupboard here I can step onto the top of. I'm going to close his attic for him, just in case vermin get down into his place from the attic while he's away. I'll go out the front door."

"Vermin?" I repeated Clive's triggering word. Even though just part of my body was protruding into the attic, he had said enough for me not to stay there any longer. Just as Clive dropped out of sight, I scurried down the ladder.

"Clive is in Raphael's apartment. He dropped down through the attic and is going out through the front door," I said, a little out of breath to the faces waiting for me; Davide, Sophia and Shadow.

"Raphael's apartment?" Sophia asked. "Isn't that the one that no one has been in?"

Davide's eyes were lighting up. "Clive was telling me about him... no one knows what he is doing in there by candlelight."

"That's the one..." The three of us looked at each other. I knew they were thinking the same as me, but I didn't want to be the first to suggest it.

Shadow was looking at us one to the other, waiting for one to make the slightest next move.

Davide gave in, spinning on his heal. "What are we waiting for? An invitation? Let's go!"

Shadow let an excited yelp and led the way, skidding down the wooden floors to the front door with the rest of us cantering after her.

"Don't close the door," we all screeched at Clive as he stood in the front doorway of Raphael's apartment, about to pull it closed after himself.

"Why?" He looked confused at us. All out of breath, we came to a screeching halt in front of him. Clive, being the gentleman in the group, having a snoop hadn't crossed his mind, obviously.

"Emmm, he borrowed something... at the party." I said at the same time as Sophia chorused, "We need to put this in the fridge," holding the bottle of wine she had grabbed off the table on the way.

"What did you bring that for?" I asked in a scolding voice, looking at the bottle in her hand.

"It would be better in his fridge than out in the heat."

"But then he'll know we were in there."

"Oh, yeah..." said the girl, who can speak six languages but sometimes gave me reason to question her thought process.

"We just want to have a quick nose Clive, now get out of the way." Davide's honesty with his new boyfriend was straight to the point.

"I'm not having anything to do with this," Clive said, holding up jazz hands as we all pushed past him. "I'm going to get my ladder."

"Don't forget to close the hatch after you," I called after him.

Inside Raphael's was a labyrinth of canvases, all in various stages of completion. Old velvet curtains hung unevenly from missing hooks and were kept roughly closed with a clothes peg. A broken easel, propped up by an empty wooden wine crate, leaned against the far wall with a slashed canvas on it. Beside it, a wooden pot stand table with a mound of melted candles formed a miniature wax city. It, in itself, could have been a work of art formed over many years except for the dust and spiderwebs.

"Wow, they weren't joking when they said he's a great artist, his work is so detailed... and classic. But none seem quite finished," said Sophia, gently thumbing through some of the piled canvases leaning against a wall.

"Maybe he has all his finished is work somewhere else, and these are just works in progress?" I said, using my more logical brain than hers again.

"So that explains the mystery. He doesn't stay here, he just uses it as a studio."

"And storage it seems," I said, referring to the various stacks of clutter on shelves and in corners that would not recognise a duster if they saw one. The bundle of dust sheets near the entrance lay ready to be thrown over his work should anyone knock.

"Nothing mysterious about this place. I'm so disappointed. I was expecting to find at least someone tied up or collections of body parts in jars," joked Davide. "There is something weird about his paintings through," he continued, trying to figure out what was different.

"I know what it is," interjected Sophia. "Everyone is turned away, none of his paintings have faces."

"That's right. He said at the dinner he does not like to paint faces."

"I suppose that is why he sticks to mostly still-life paintings.... This one looks familiar I'm sure I've seen it somewhere before... in an art book or a gallery... Actually I recognise several of these... Shadow stop!" shouted Sophia taking giant steps towards Shadow who had her head tucked behind two teetering canvases leaning up against the walls about to topple with her clumsy body moving further in behind to get at whatever it was she was chasing or trying to eat.

While she dealt with Shadow, I looked through the canvases Sophia had been browsing through and I recognised several too. They were all copies.

"I can see what he means about not being good at faces. This kid's face is odd looking, something about the eyes." Sophia picked up a canvas out of Shadow's tongue's reach.

"That's the Ugly Child painting!" I could see it from where I stood.

"I wouldn't say it's that bad," said Davide, looking over Sophia's shoulder. "I mean she's not a bunch of roses but it's harsh calling a child ugly... actually on second thoughts you are right, she is ugly as hell."

"That painting is of Ciara when she was a kid. Paolo's grandmother painted it. It's hanging in the room I'm staying in, well, it was until yesterday. How did it get here? I just saw it in the attic... Oh hang on, it's not the same. This one has a dog," I noted, looking closer at the painting. "Raphael must have copied it... how strange." With that, we heard steps on the flagstones outside. "Shoot he's coming! Hide!"

21

David leapt behind the front door swiping the bottle of wine as he went and flattened himself against the wall. His pale blue suit actually made him blend in, camouflaged against the sky of the mural seascape on the wall. I wasn't too sure if his aim in grabbing the wine was to hide the evidence that we were there, or if he was planning to use the bottle as a weapon, or possibly drink it while waiting. Sophia disappeared into the next room as fast as a hare. While Shadow and I wrapped ourselves behind the long burgundy velvet curtain. I held my breath.

"Hello, is anyone here?" I immediately recognised the voice. Shadow did too and her tail, which I then realised was sticking out from beneath the curtain, began to sweep the floor back and forth rapidly.

"Surprise Happy Birthday Raphael!" screeched Davide, popping out from behind the door brandishing the bottle of wine.

I pushed back the curtain and was relieved that the familiar voice was Paolo's and that it was not Raphael standing at the door. "Davide, what are you... what are you both doing in here? It's Raphael's birthday?"

"No, that was just a bluff. I barely remember what Raphael looks like, never mind when his birthday is. I was desperate though. What else could I say?" Davide was to be commended for his effort of covering up our lack of good hiding skills.

"That does not explain why you are all in here, though?" said Paolo, standing in the open door.

"I'll leave that to your girlfriend to explain," said Davide, twitching his head in my direction. "Clive and I only came to collect the ladder. I'll see you kids later." And off Davide went across the walkway towards Ciara's house carrying the bottle of wine, with me shouting after him, "I'm not his girlfriend."

Paolo was still in the authoritative policeman stance. He was spending way too long amongst his old kind, and it was beginning to show. "Well?" he said, as if I owed him an explanation of why we were in someone else's house.

"None of your damn business, actually. You are not a cop now, remember? Or are you? You still haven't explained yourself..." I couldn't see his reaction as his body was in silhouette against the doorway and my hair had got caught in the clothes peg while I was trying to escape from the dusty curtains.

"Perhaps if you agreed to be my girlfriend..." he said, coming over to help me untangle me.

"Anyway," I interrupted, not wanting to go down that rabbit hole. "Never mind why we are here, Paolo. Did they arrest Valentino?"

I was at last freed and Shadow had backed up and got herself out from under the curtain. Between the bunch of hair stuck in the peg and Shadow's tail dusting skills, we were going to have to come up with a good explanation to Raphael of why we had been in his apartment. There was too much evidence now to cover up.

"No, I didn't make it to the station. I was on my way to the car and Ciara called me to say she had collected Valentino and they were stopping off for lunch on the way home. Then I realised I'd forgotten my wallet, so I came back to get money for a parking meter. I didn't want to come back with a parking fine on your car."

"Oh right. Coming back with a murderer is a much better idea than coming back with a parking fine." He didn't miss out on my sarcasm.

"Seriously though, why are you and Davide in here? Is Raphael back, I think they will want to talk with him again down at the station?" Paolo couldn't help himself flicking through some canvases.

"It's a long story. Clive was collecting his ladder from Ciara's. He got up in the attic. He saw Raphael's attic door was open and decided it would be best to close it in case of creepy things and opened the front door and... well, we all came to.... Make sure the place was secure and... never mind, look what we found..." I held up the canvas for Paolo to see. "He copied the Ugly Child painting..."

"Why would he copy that? Except he's put a pup in his one, there's a flower in her hand in Ciara's one... Maybe Ciara asked him to?" He stroked the glistening area on the painting gently and checked his finger tips for fresh paint. I didn't have the heart to tell him it was Shadow's slobber.

"To copy a painting she hates? I don't think so." I was voicing my thoughts as I tried to make sense of it myself.

"Wait... did you say Clive came in here from Ciara's attic?" I nodded at his question. "If you can go from one attic to another, then it could have been anyone in this building that put the wire up there, not just Valentino."

I put the reason to why I hadn't thought of that yet, down to the excitement of having a nosey in the mysterious apartment, but now I was thinking about it. "How far away was the wire from the hatch door where you found it?... Ciara had said Valentino had looked into the attic... I don't think he would be physically able enough to climb in and out of it with his bad hip."

Paolo was about to answer me, but was interrupted by a more urgent voice.

"Guys," called Sophia from the door into the adjacent room. "The Ugly Child is not the only painting he copied. Look in here."

"Sophia is here too?" said Paolo, looking in disbelief at Sophia who was now standing in the doorway of the next room up the hallway, "Unbelievable!"

"You're not in the police force anymore, remember?" I shrugged off his disapproving tone, as I pushed past him and hurried to see what Sophia had found.

In the room's corner where Sophia had been hiding and we forgot to tell her it was safe to come out, was a pile of canvases all the same size. All of them had The Vase of Flowers painting at different stages. Two were slashed. "He obviously wasn't too happy how those attempts were turning out," smirked Sophia.

"He did the forgery of The Vase of Flowers," I yelped. "Crap, we really shouldn't be in here as they are criminal evidence, right Paolo?"

"I am not sure if what he did could be classed as a crime. From what I've heard he kept telling people he didn't believe it was the original... but by constantly saying the negative he kept people arguing the positive, trying to prove his denial wrong... But it doesn't add up, Valentino or Ciara told us that Raphael didn't collect the finders reward even when everyone thought it was the original, before the isotope test was discovered."

"Why would he do the forgery if he wasn't doing it for the money?" asked Sophia, equally confused, looking through the pile of canvases.

"That might not be a crime... but this could prove he did one, and one more serious than forgery," I said, looking at the wall behind our backs.

Leaning against the other wall were five of the same painting all with slightly different facial features. A woman lay on a chaise longue with pearls hanging from her hand.

"He was painting her," whispered Paolo.

"There was no secret about that. At the party, he openly said he was working on a project with her..."

"But this was the pose she was found in," continued Paolo. "He didn't mention he was working with her that day during questioning. And I thought she only posed for Filippo now, since they started being a couple..."

It was then I noticed the package behind the door of the room in a carrier bag, ready to be brought somewhere. Wrapped similarly to the package left on the doorstep for Ciara and Valentino two days ago.

On it was an old-fashioned luggage tag with perfect calligraphy styled hand writing; 'Private and Confidential. For the attention of Filippo Garcia.' I tore it open before anyone could tell me not to. Inside was a bubble-wrapped canvas. On it was the Woman with Pearls.

22

"I think it's the original of Klimt's painting the Woman with Pearls that Valentino mentioned." I wasn't sure if it was the awe of holding a priceless masterpiece by my favourite artist in my hands or the touch of Paolo's breath on that little sensitive spot I have between my shoulder and neck that was making my hands tremble. "You hold it, I'm afraid I'll drop it," I said, shoving it into the care of Paolo's firm grip.

"How did he get his hands on that... And what's this?" asked Sophia, pulling out a padded envelope from the bag. Again it was addressed to Filippo with Private and Confidential written on it. Which I promptly ignored.

"Wait, you can't-" said Paolo, as I ripped open the top of the envelop.

"You're not a cop now, remember?" I knew I was taunting him, but it was working to my advantage at that moment. He could either claim he was and stop me in my tracks or say nothing, which gave me free rein to do what I wished. I tapped the side of the envelop and out fell some old tubes of paint and brushes, wrapped in a note. 'In the event that it needs touching up. Keep her safe and in time please do the honourable thing with this masterpiece.'

Looking at the painting in Paolo's hands and looking at the tubes of paints dabbed with long hardened chunks of similar colours used in the painting, it wasn't difficult for us to come to the same conclusion.

"So, it's not the original, it's one of his forgeries," said Paolo. "But just in case I think we should get Valentino to check it out."

"I'd like to get out of here, it's creeping me out." A visible shiver went up Sophia's spine as she said the words. "What if he is the murderer and comes back, finds us here and murders us all."

"I'd like to see him try..." I said, feeling defensive. "But yes, I get you. I'm feeling a bit creeped out myself. Let's go back to Ciara's and have a cup of tea. We can get back in through the attic if we need to get in again."

"More tea? I think I'd rather stay here and chance being murdered," groaned Sophia.

"You can have water then! Tea is not compulsory, but I feel it helps fix things."

"Super glue works better, I find." Paolo was back in joking form and out of his imaginary police uniform.

"Should we take this with us?" I waved my hand at the Klimt painting Paolo had rested on an empty easel that was plastered in a colourful selection of paint layers over the years. Beside it rested the spillage of paint tubes from the padded envelope.

"No, it's best to leave these here as evidence if needed. I'll get on to Emanuele down at the station and get him to come here to collect the wire rather than me bring it in. I can show them the location I found it. It will be significant in getting Valentino off the hook too. I think it would have been out of his reach to throw it from the hatch door. And as you said before, I don't think he would have been able to climb fully into the attic with his bad hip."

We walked quietly out of the room, as if not wanting to disturb the dead. The canvases in the entrance room with the blocked out natural light now had an eerie presence about them.

Paolo and I paused to have a last look at the piles of paintings.

"I'll go put on the kettle for you and your tea addiction," Sophia said without stopping, but instead quickening her step. She'd had enough.

"So here's another question I have..." I said to the listening ears of Paolo and Shadow. "Why did Raphael bother to do forgeries? With the isotope tests, he couldn't market the fake master pieces he created. Like the Vase of Flowers. It looked perfect but didn't pass the isotope test. Also, with him doing forgeries of missing works of art, the original could still be found, especially if someone was hiding it and heard an imposter painting claiming to be the original turned up... just like the Vase of Flowers original came to light."

"I don't know," said Paolo, bending over slightly to scratch the ear of Shadow, who was pressing herself up against his leg. She only did that to me. A flitting flicker of jealously found itself forming the words, 'how dare they be so close' in my head, but I cleared my throat and focused on what Paolo had to say.

"What we have learned now is that Filippo knows more about this than he has said so far. He's involved. I don't know how yet, but he is definitely as knee deep in this as Raphael is. When I call Detective Emanuele, I will tell him... I mean will suggest to him... to bring Filippo and Raphael in for questioning again, specifically about the painting. I'll also... suggest they get a warrant to search both this apartment and Filippo's," Paolo said.

"I am sure the detective will follow your... suggestions... you being just a good citizen and all that." I was being snarky, and he knew it, but didn't honour me with a response, and instead gazed at the canvas Shadow was licking earlier.

"What I don't understand is why he forged Aunt Ciara's Ugly Child painting? My grandmother was a good hobby artist but not a grand master. Not even the original is of value, never mind a forgery."

"It's not even a good forgery... it's different. An improvement actually, but still weird." The sound of footsteps echoed in the courtyard below as the front wooden gate creaked closed and the chatter of Aunt Ciara and Valentino drifted up. They had stopped to greet Davide and Clive carrying the ladder–on their way to demolish the offending ivy at the restaurant.

"Perhaps your aunt asked him to improve it?" It was the only explanation I could come up with.

"There's only one way to find out. Come on," Paolo said, grasping his knapsack in one hand, still with the murder weapon in it and the Ugly Child in the other. Striding across the portico to Aunt Ciara's open door, we could hear the kettle whistle coming to a crescendo. It was not just the water that was coming to a boil.

23

"Oh yes, a cup of tea would be lovely," said Valentino, answering my offer, completely unaware that we had him branded as a cold-blooded murderer less than an hour ago. Had both he and Paolo not forgotten their wallets that morning, he would now be locked up in prison, waiting for his lawyer to arrive.

"Did you have a look at my dress?" Ciara gave me a sidewards you-can-tell-me smile. Like Valentino, she did not know that Paolo and I were so close to collapsing her world and bursting her bubble of happiness less than an hour ago. With everything that had just happened, I completely drew a blank as to what she was referring to. I must have looked guilty, as she immediately continued. "I don't mind if you did. I can imagine you are dying to see it, with the Irish lace connection and everything. And I did find a lucky shamrock in the pattern like you said."

"Wow, I didn't realise those things worked," Sophia spurted out, taking the cups from the shelf.

"Oh no... I didn't look at your dress. I wanted to wait until you modelled it so I told Sophia to put it away... hide it... carefully... so I wouldn't be tempted."

Sophia was eyeballing me like never before. Her eyes flickered to the small cupboard under the TV and back to my eyes. My eyelids felt they were sucked back and my eyeballs bulging. Had she squashed all the bags in there? I know I said to hide them, but how the hell did she fit them all in there?

"Paolo, perhaps you could take Shadow and Valentino for a quick walk?"

"What? N-"

Before he could finish his 'No' he realised by my glare that there was no chance of ever calling me girlfriend if didn't take this hint. I needed to get them out of sight so that Sophia could retrieve the bags from their squashed hiding place.

"I think there is a certain dress to be viewed that you are not allowed to see Valentino, let's take a quick walk and then have that cup of tea... without milk." Paolo got his dig in.

As soon as they exited with a more than excited Shadow weaving between them, herding them out, I piped up, "Okay Ciara, why don't you get into the bedroom and get ready to model the dress."

"Fantastic. I know just the lingerie I want to wear under it. A French knicker set, Valentino bought me in Paris on our first trip away last year. Is the dress in my wardrobe?"

"Yes, it is! Off you go and put on that... lingerie." The only lingerie I had bought in the last 20 years was five packs of cotton bikini briefs 'in a variety of holiday colours' and discounted ill-fitting bras from Primark the last time I was back in Ireland. My sex life was obviously far less adequate than this woman nearly twice my age. Which would have been perfectly fine if I was 14 rather than 45. I made a mental note to myself to step up my underwear game.

As soon as the closing latch hit its receiver in her door, Sophia dived for the cabinet and, with difficulty, pulled out the resistant shopping bags she had crammed in. "Seriously? In such a small space?" I said as the creased-up bags landed on the rug.

"What could I do, it was an emergency," defended Sophia.

"Ciara," I called, standing outside her door with the bags and Sophia, after tapping on the door. "Sorry, I thought Sophia had put the bags in your room but she... placed them in my room.... Silly billy."

"Sure, bring them in," she called out.

Coyly, we approached the bed like it was a sleeping tiger we were trying to harness.

"What do you think?" said Ciara as she swished out of her ensuite in an open, knee length silk robe with matching lace trimmed French knickers and balcony bra. Her lightly tanned, wrinkled skin looked like a landscape of vineyards or a geological map of a volcanic island. It had history, it was wise, and it had a story to tell. She looked stunning, but not like I ever imagined beauty before.

Her reaction to seeing the bags broke my trance, though. "Oh Dio, what happened to the bags?" She said, rushing over to them as if they were a sack of puppies left on the side of a motorway.

"I fell..." spurted out Sophia. "On top of them.. The bags... as I was running up the steps outside. Tripped on my shoelace," she said glancing down at her footwear and realising she was wearing sandals, "I mean my sole... I tripped over my loose sole..." Again I felt my eyeballs bulging as I watched Ciara hoping she would believe the crap pouring out of Sophia's mouth. Sophia lied so well she probably did have a loose soul. Ciara didn't need to consider it, Sophia was a pure angel in her eyes.

"Oh my goodness, you should have said. I'm glad you didn't tumble down the stairs. They are very uneven. I am used to them, but I should warn visitors about the worn parts. Come to think of it, I am probably the one in the complex that has caused the worn parts the most. I've been here since I was about ten, longer than anyone else! Although I am starting to find the steps difficult now," she said, pulling out an emerald green stripped square box from the biggest bag and shaking off the lid. "Close your eyes," she ordered excitedly as she unfolded the gold tissue paper inside.

"Okay, you can open your eyes now." She stood in front of the body length mirror with the simple but beautiful, knee-length ivory dress loosely outlining her slender figure.

I had been to many dress fittings over my twenty years of wedding planning, but for some reason, Ciara struck me speechless. She was spectacular.

"You look absolutely stunning."

"Thank you, Daisy. And as a little thank for helping us plan the wedding, I bought you a little something too." She pushed a smaller, now very crinkled, bag from the same shop over to the side of the bed I was sitting on. Inside, folded in lime green tissue paper, was a cream lace cardigan with three quarter length sleeves delicately finished with a scallop edge.

"Oh Ciara you shouldn't have... it's beautiful."

"Sophia said you had a powder blue linen dress that she thought you might decide to wear to the wedding," she said, pulling open her free standing mirror to reveal a jewellery cabinet inside. "I was going to get you a pure white one, but then I thought you might look like the Virgin Mary, so we decided cream was best. Try it on, we can bring it back and get something else if it doesn't fit or if you don't like it."

There was nothing not to like about it. It fitted perfectly and softened my stressed face. I hadn't realised how tense I was until I caught my own vision in the mirror, but who wouldn't be after the last few hours.

"Ah yes, perfect what do you think ladies?" said Ciara as she turned to face us with a long string of pearls tied in a loose knot just below her chest. Although it was not a flapper dress, the pearls gave it a subtle touch of 1920s elegance.

"Perfect," Sophia and I said in unison.

"Great, that's me dressed for the wedding. Now let's have that tea."

24

"Have they told you about Raphael?" Valentino was tripping over his words he was trying to get them out so fast when they returned from their mandatory man walk.

"No, we were too busy discussing dresses to talk about anything else. What's happened, does he want the painting he gave us back, because he can-"

"He's the murderer!" blurted out Valentino.

"We don't know that yet, but-" intervened Paolo.

"And he was the one that forged the Vase of Flowers painting." Valentino continued enthusiastically, ignoring Paolo's interruption. "And others. That's what he is doing over there cooped up in his apartment. Being a lean, mean, forging machine."

"Goodness... are you sure?" Ciara pulled the top sides of her cardigan together as if that would protect her from the murderer at large.

"No, we are not sure. As I said, we don't know yet if he committed the murder-" Paolo was getting exasperated.

"No, I mean about the Vase of Flowers. Are we sure he did it?"

"Emm yes..." I could see Paolo was as confused as I was about Ciara being more concerned about Raphael forging her favourite painting than having a murderer living in the apartment just flagstones away.

"The lying bugger," she eased herself into her chair at the table where the rest of us were now sitting, helping ourselves to the pot of tea.

"I've called detective Emanuele, and he is coming here later today to search his apartment. They are just waiting for the search warrant to be granted. But please do not say this to anyone," urged Paolo.

Ciara made a little closing zip movement across her lips.

Strangely, I was no longer that concerned about who was the murderer either, but more curious about something odd. "Ciara," I said, taking another sip of my tea before getting up and bringing the canvas that had been resting in the hall over to the table. "We found this copy of the Ugly Child painting in Raphael's apartment. We are trying to figure out why he'd copy it. Did you ask him to?"

"That's not a copy dear," Ciara stated matter-of-factly, taking the canvas in her hands. "My mother did two paintings of me. This one was the ugliest. Poor Fufu looks demented in it. I loved that dog... but this picture of him is awful. That's why I kept it in the attic with my mother's art equipment. He was perfectly darling, but she portrayed him like a vicious dog. Like he was guarding something."

She paused to look at the painting more closely.

"I never understood why she insisted on painting on old canvases. But I suppose in those days you just had to take what you were given. There were no cheap art supply shops then. I always remember Georgio bringing in a stack of canvases to my mother and her painting these hideous portraits like crazy for days after.

"I asked her why she painted me so ugly and she laughed, saying she had sacrificed my good looks so that the Nazi's wouldn't see them as worth taking... No fear of the Nazis wanting these paintings of an ugly child by a random woman trying to paint her kid. I felt insulted they didn't take them when they did come and search our house."

Ciara put the canvas down on the floor, leaning against the wall beside her.

"The day Georgio delivered the canvases... he wasn't his usual cheerful self, he was frantic. I think he knew he was going to be captured. He kissed my mother goodbye, and she wept. She immediately started painting, while still weeping. I suppose art must have been a stress relief for her. That was the last time we saw Georgio. A few days later we heard they had taken him to one of the camps."

A sense of sadness fell across the room. Ciara returned her attention to her teacup.

"Aunt Ciara," said Paolo softly, "I was in the attic this morning and Grandmother's art equipment was up not there. Only the dinner service and now the other Ugly Child painting."

"Nonsense. Her art stuff is definitely up there. Her paint brushes, easel, paints, canvases. On the right just as you go up. I put them there myself. Valentino, did you see them when you were up there?"

"I only looked into the attic, but I do not recall any art materials."

"Shadow stop!" I interrupted. Shadow was licking the Ugly Child painting like crazy. "Ciara, you might not like that painting, but Shadow seems to love Fufu."

"She must still taste the honey. My mother used to use honey from our farm to make thinners for her paints. It was the most delicious honey ever. I would lick the painting myself if it meant I would taste it again."

"Shadow stop it, look at your tongue..." I said, getting up to lift the painting away from her. "Oh no I'm sorry Ciara. Shadow has licked off some of the paint..." I said, embarrassed at my big oaf of a dog's behaviour, but then I got distracted. "Wow, that looks colourful," I said, picking up the canvas where Shadow had pinned little ugly Ciara and Fufu into the corner. A rich red and corner of gold showed through the bland beige and white's of Fufu's fur.

"Oh My!" said Ciara. "Mother painted over a painting. I wonder what it is, it's bound to be more interesting than the one she did. Valentino, if you are not too tired, shall we take it over to the restoration studios to get x-rayed?"

"Absolutely, this is exciting!" Valentino said, wiping his mouth with a napkin.

"Can I come I'd love to see how it works?" Sophia asked.

"Of course! You can all come if you like."

"I won't go as I am waiting on..." hesitated Paolo, "on the delivery of your wedding gift."

It was true that Paolo had a wedding present package being delivered by a courier from Rome later that day. After several glasses of wine the previous evening, he had spent an hour on the phone with his friend who was house sitting his plants for the week. "I'm getting a perfect wedding present sent up from Rome for Aunt Ciara," he had explained, but refused to give me any more information about it other than it's going to be the best present ever.

However, I knew the real reason he was staying at the apartment. He was waiting for detective Emanuele to arrive–to hand over the murder weapon. And hopefully, by showing him where he found it, Paolo would get Valentino removed from the suspect list.

On our way out the gate, Davide and Clive were returning. The centre wrung of the ladder perched with ease on Clive's shoulder while Davide followed behind shouting be-careful instructions at him so he wouldn't bang the unseen end of the ladder on the entrance.

I dropped back from the enthusiastic bunch as they all walked arm in arm out the gate towards the Uffizi studios. "Guys, would you mind bringing the ladder back to Paolo, he's in the apartment. I think he's going to need it again."

"Of course, I will bring it straight there and put it up for him. The catch on it is a little tricky," agreed Clive, barely stopping.

Over at the restoration studios, it was apparent the x-ray machine wasn't used very often as it was currently being used as a shelf space to store documents for shredding.

It didn't take long to have it cleared off and for Valentino to place the Ugly Child in position. We stood waiting, staring at the screen in the observation room as the light loomed back and forth, taking a look inside the ugly child.

"No doubt it's one of Georgio's castoffs, but this is fun all the same. Perhaps it will be a portrait of my mother or at least one that she posed for."

But when the x-ray image became clear on the screen, Valentino's glasses fell off the end of his nose as he nearly head butted the screen to verify what he was looking at. "Oh Dio, it can't be... Ciara, are you seeing what I am seeing..." They both glared at the screen in disbelief.

25

"My God..." said Ciara to the screen from her seat centre stage. "Have I had Klimt's Woman with Pearls in my attic all this time?"

"Perhaps it's just a copy, something your mother was practising?" said Valentino, trying to cover all the possibilities before allowing himself to get excited.

"It makes sense now," said Ciara, tapping her finger on the desk. "She painted over it, to hide it from the Nazis. That is why she made me so ugly, so the Nazis wouldn't take it. Georgio... Georgio brought her the canvases that morning. That is why she had to paint over them so quickly..."

They all glared at the hidden woman lying on the chaise longue behind the Ugly Child and it then struck me.

"Ciara," I said cautiously, not wanting anyone to have a heart attack at what I was about to say. "You said he was carrying several paintings that morning... how many?... The other Ugly Child painting... now in the attic..." I had suddenly lost the ability to string words together in a cohesive sentence, but they knew exactly what I meant.

"Call Paolo and tell him to bring it over immediately," urged Valentino, finding himself a chair. "Tell him to bring the bottle of brandy too. I need a stiff drink... I need to call some people, get them here and get this secured and verified. Oh Dio, Dio, Dio..."

I stepped outside the room into the hallway. A shiver crawled up my back, making my hands tremble a little as I pressed Paolo's name on my phone screen. It was the same hallway we had entered the other studio from only days ago and found Julia. It seemed a lifetime ago. The hours since then had been filled to the brim, jammed with details. It took a few moments for Paolo to answer.

"Emanuele and his team have just left the apartment and are searching Raphael's apartment now. Emanuele agrees Valentino would not have been able to throw the wire to where I found it. The angle is wrong... it must have been Raphael who put it there. They have brought Filippo in for more questioning, but Raphael seems to have gone missing. Anna said she hasn't seen him since she got out of the police station two nights ago and she is quite frantic as he hasn't answered her calls since then either." Paolo said all this between quick panting breaths, before I could even say 'hello.'

"Why are you so out of breath?"

"Sorry, I have you on speakerphone. I'm just taking this damn ladder down, it's so bloody awkward. But it's done now, I can talk properly to you."

"Hang on, you need to put it back up."

"You are joking..."

"No, I am serious. You need to get back up in the attic and get the Ugly Child over here as fast as possible... but handle it with care... great care."

"You mean the painting I flung into the attic, yesterday?" The word flung made me wince. I winced even more at the memory of me bashing it with the door, trying to get out of the bathroom when it had fallen off the wall and Shadow nearly devouring it.

"Actually, maybe get Emanuele to give you a police escort over here with it." Even though I was no art expert, I was starting to feel the surge of excitement at the hidden treasure that might lie beneath. "Paolo, the x-ray showed... well, it showed what looks like the original Woman with Pearls... behind the other Ugly Child, the one in the attic might be hiding another priceless painting." Saying it made me think deeper about it and push the pieces of the jigsaw together. "That's why Raphael felt confident no one would find the original of his forgery this time... Because he knew it was behind the Ugly Child... he must have found it in the attic... that's why he wanted to snoop around your Aunt's apartment, to see if he could find anymore of your grandmother's paintings."

"I'm sure you are making perfect sense Daisy but I'm... a bit... busy... struggling with this ladder again." His voice was straining. I made a mental note that if we ever did move in together, we would probably need to get tradespeople in to do everything, as Paolo couldn't even figure out how to put a ladder up.

"I'll explain better when you get over here. Just be really careful with that painting, cover it and get an armed guard to come with you, just in case Raphael shows up or word has somehow got out. "

"I don't need an armed guard. I'll just bring Shadow."

Why hadn't I thought of Shadow? She would be much better protection than any armed guard and if someone did nab the painting she'd be able to chase after them and have them pinned to the ground quicker than any human.

"Yes, you are right, and she should be here and part of the excitement. After all, she was the one who discovered the hidden masterpiece."

Back in the x-ray room, Valentino was busy chattering on the phone, rounding up his ancient team of restorers and the Looters Committee, or whatever they were called. Sophia was listening attentively to Ciara's explanation of the Nazi's art stealing episode during the war.

"Okay," Valentino said, carefully retrieving the Ugly Child and Fufu the dog from the machine. "I'm afraid Ciara, the restoration team will need to clean off the paint from the painting. Which will mean your mother's painting of you and your dog will be destroyed."

"I aways hated it. There were so many times I was very close to throwing it out." The words rolled off her tongue before she gripped her pout. "To think I was going to throw it... them out... the very things I have dedicated most of my life searching for and they were there in front of me all this time. How disastrously ironic that would have been."

"Well, they weren't in front of you, they were behind you," I couldn't help but joke. "Behind the back of you as an Ugly Child. You have been protecting them ever since then without even knowing."

She sighed "I know they are ugly but I'm going to miss them now all the same."

"Let's not get too excited," said Valentino, again protecting his emotions. "Perhaps there will be nothing significant behind the other. You might still be able to keep the other painting untouched. If so, we should hang it in a place with more honour, I think, wouldn't you agree?"

With that Paolo came bustling in with an old string cobweb still stuck to his back, a red faced out of breath Detective Emanuele following him and an excited Shadow by his leg. "Shadow made us jog all the way here. I nearly dropped it at one point." Paolo said, referring to the rectangular flat parcel he had crudely wrapped with the string and brown paper the Vase of Flowers gift had arrived in.

"Perhaps Shadow knows more than any of us about what lies behind the Ugly Child. Hand it here and let's have a look," smiled Valentino. He lifted the first Ugly Child to a cleared table as if he was carrying a tray of liquid gold, before placing the next Ugly Child on the machine ready for her examination.

Back at the screen it became quite clear that there was a painting lurking underneath, but that wasn't what caused my chest to cave in from loss of shocked breath. The fright was that I recognised the figure emerging.

26

"It's the girl from my nightmares, the one trying to get out of the attic, where's that brandy?" I exclaimed as the image became clear on the screen.

"And mine!" gasped Ciara. "It's the ghostly-looking girl that has being haunting my nights too! But now I know who it is... why hadn't I recognised her before? It's not a girl from a nightmare, it's a girl of our dreams." She was more excited about this discovery than the last.

"It is Trudie Steiner by Klimt," explained Valentino. He was clicking on the magnifying button with quick snaps of his finger. "It was another piece of artwork that was confiscated by the Nazis. They took it from Trudie Steiner's family home following her parents' escape. The painting hasn't been seen since it was sold to a mysterious buyer in 1941."

"Perhaps Georgio was the mystery person who bought the paintings at the auctions? To protect them? He must have known the Nazis would come after him for them when they discovered who the mysterious buyer was and that is why he left the canvases in my mother's care."

"What about Trudie, did she survive the war?" Sophia asked in her undulating, caring tone, while we all looked at the ghostly image on the screen.

"She never made it to the war years," stated Valentino. "This is a ghost painting–a portrait painted of Trudie following her death when she was just a teenager. Klimt did it before he became famous in Vienna."

"She may be a ghost now, but the painting of her is no longer a ghost. We have found it. Or should we say Shadow led us to it." Paolo gave a happy, panting Shadow a playful rub on the ear and she looked up at him adoringly. They were becoming too attached.

Detective Emanuele's phone buzzed, and he stepped outside to take it.

"I know they are ugly but I'm going to miss them now all the same," sighed Ciara, watching Valentino through the glass panel carefully place the two ugly identical twins side by side.

"Why don't I slip in and take some photos with my phone before they go? They'll look great in your wedding photo album."

"Yes please. But we won't be doing a photo album," said Ciara with a chuckle. We could hear the murmur of feet and voices coming up the stairs down the hall.

I did some quick snaps before the excited experts got to the room to stop me.

"Don't worry, the team will take high-quality photos for records and I'll get copies for Ciara. These Ugly Children and Ciara's mother will go down in art history as heroes." Valentino stood proudly, looking at them as if they were his own kids graduating, before the door flung open and a gaggle of very excited ancients whom I'd seen at the birthday party poured in. I disappeared back into the hallway where Paolo was in head bobbing whispers with Detective Emanuele. He lifted his head and, with the kindest smile, ushered me over to be part of their huddle.

"Detective Emanuele just heard from his partner at the station, Filippo has spilled the cannellini's."

"You mean beans, he spilled the beans." I stated correcting his English that he seemed to switch to whenever he wanted to use a saying that would help me understand.

"Whatever you say," said Paolo, dismissing my correction. "Raphael had done the painting, but he needed Filippo's help with the face. He had a photo from the x-ray machine of the Woman with Pearls and Filippo had been mentoring Raphael to get the face perfect. The photo lacked some detail, so they had Julia model for them to get the light right, as she had a similar shape and hair colour to the woman in the painting. Raphael had told Filippo, that he knew on good authority that the original would never be found. He also had a supply of several old canvases and a box of paints. The box had an inscription on it 'SP FERRARI'... my grandmother's paints and canvases. Raphael must have stolen them from the attic."

"Of course!" I said, now armed with the last piece of the puzzle, "your grandmother's art materials were pre-atomic bomb time so no isotopes. Making them perfect for forgeries... That must have been the noise your Aunt Ciara was hearing from the attic. It was Raphael helping himself to the antique paint supplies. What about him... has he turned up yet?"

Detective Emanuele shook his head. "We have put the word out throughout Italy. There are fingerprints all over the murder weapon, we are just waiting on confirmation that they are his... but he is now officially wanted for murder."

Shadow pushed open the observation door after hearing my voice in the hallway. Or was it Paolo who she was looking for? Ciara and Sophia followed her out of the room.

"I don't know about anyone else, but I have had enough excitement for one day," said Ciara, looking tired. "Now that Trudie has been found, she might let us sleep easy in our beds and stop banging around in the attic. Sophia has been telling me everything that is planned for tomorrow. You girls really know what you are doing."

"It's nearly all Sophia's work. I've been... distracted. Sophia has been playing a blinder, doing all the follow-up calls and fine tuning the events while I have been herding Ugly Children and been spooked by ghosts."

"Sophia is walking me home, and I'm going to have a nap and a bubble bath. We have a big day tomorrow, don't forget Detective," Ciara chirped. "The Vase of Flowers is being revealed and I'm getting married!" And off Sophia and Ciara trotted like an old married couple.

Paolo and I walked the long way back to the apartment, wandering down some of my favourite streets I enjoyed getting lost in. My hand in his. "You seemed to have warmed to Valentino or at least you seem more accepting of them getting married."

"Yeah, I was being cynical, thinking it was about money or something. But it turns out, they are just simply in love and don't want to be apart anymore. A man in love with a woman and wanting to spend the rest of his with her, it's not so difficult to understand, is it?"

"Of course," I said, and as soon as the words left my mouth I regretted it. "AHA!" he jumped in front of me with all the whites of his eyes and teeth showing like some mad version of the Joker. "So you DO believe in love and marriage!"

"Oh, stop it Paolo. I believe in love and yes, I think for... some people... marriage is a great thing. But it will never be for me. To be honest, I am not sure why your aunt and Valentino are getting married at this stage."

"Listen to you now. You sound like everyone else," laughed Paolo. Our path had led us back to the banks of the Arno, where we automatically sat down together on a patch of grass. Two white swans landed in perfect unison on the silver ripples before furling their wings back against their bodies like neatly stacked linen and gliding away as mirrors of each other.

"I mean, why don't they just continue how they are? It's not like they are intending to have kids or already have big families and need an excuse for a celebration to get them all to reunite." I sat with my arms wrapped around my knees, Paolo by my side, propped up by his elbow. "Well, there is a practical reason for it too. They had a long serious conversation about it with me at the party." He chewed on a grass blade, his eyes squinting in the early evening sun.

"Ciara is moving in to Valentino's place. A cushy little villa estate just over on that hill," he said, pointing to the other side of the river. "In Fiesole."

"I know Fiesole, I have a wedding there this summer in Castello Vincigliata."

"Well, it sounds like he has a good setup. He has a cook and live-in help. Aunt Ciara is finding the apartment steps a little tiring and so they are thinking ahead. If she moves in with him without getting married, then things could get complicated if something should happen to him. Once married, if he should die first, then Aunt Ciara would inherit it and could stay there with no potential complication should a distant relative lay claim to Valentino's fortune."

"Yes, there was no mention of children or relatives on the guest list they did up yesterday. I was wondering..."

"He never had kids, never married... I think he might still be a virgin." In his dead pan voice, the last statement was all the funnier as I let myself fall back and lie beside him on the grass, taking a moment to watch a wisp of cloud disappear and become one with the blue.

"So, what will happen to her apartment?"

"It reverts to me. That guy Georgio left it to my grandmother, who left it to my mother and to Ciara as long as Ciara wanted to live there... It was odd how she worded the will, perhaps she just presumed my mother being the youngest would outlive Ciara. But basically I inherited my mother's half and now that Ciara is moving out, it becomes fully mine."

"Oh... what will you do with it?"

"I have had little time to think about it, but I am thinking of moving in and using it as an office base."

"An office base?" I sat up again. He had my full attention. "For what business?"

"Okay, it's time for me to come clean and tell you something... even though you are not my girlfriend... yet... wait, let me check first... are we going out together?"

"No, we are not. You haven't even asked me on a date," I said with laughter bubbling up.

"Oh, come on, was the trip to the Sistine Chapel not a date?"

"NO, that was my suggestion. I'm an old-fashioned girl when it comes to some things and technically you have not asked me on a date yet... Now get on with what you were going to tell me."

I could see he was thinking about a solution, but he went on with what he had to tell me, anyway.

"After my Olympic dreams were dashed, I joined the police force when I was 19-"

"Hang on, you were an athlete?"

"Yes, I rowed like that guy," he said, nodding towards a rower streaking past on the surface of the Arno. "Oh, so you are the sports person the Tarot card reader told me about!" I had blurted out the words before I could stop myself.

"What are you talking about?"

"Oh nothing, it was something that happened before we met in Rome. Sorry, carry on I want to hear your story." I realised I had interrupted him enough for him to be reconsidering whether he should tell me his well-kept secret. "Please tell me."

"From the police force, I progressed to being a detective in the mafia squad... undercover... I never left. They placed me as an agent in the Russi hotel chain to flush out a money laundering scam under the guise of being a hotel manager.

"It was supposed to be a quick operation, but it went on for the last five years. There was a much bigger, linked operation going on. Massive in fact. You will hear about it soon in the news but let's say Italy will be a better place for it. Anyway, my work is now done on that operation. They want me to start on a new one but... It's not what I want to do. I want to start having a quiet life. So I am thinking of setting up my own private detective agency... find missing dogs or uncovering insurance scams, small stuff, you know? I don't want to be hunting down people like Raphael, who knows when they'll find him, it could go on for years." He wasn't looking for my approval. He picked up another grass stem and played with it in his mouth before chewing on the end. "And maybe find a woman to love uncontrollably, grow vegetables together, go for walks along a lake front perhaps..." He looked at me, the grass stem in the corner of his mouth rose slightly with the corner of his lips.

"Well, that rules me out." I said, sighing loudly.

He looked at me with his big teddy bear eyes, "Well I wasn't talking about you," he blurted with a glint in his eye, "but just for curiosity, why would you not be a contender?"

"Because every time we meet each other, we find a dead body. That is far from a quiet life. No, no, no, I wouldn't fit in with that life at all," I smirked. "But I am interested in your business. I think it's a great idea. You'd make a brilliant Private Dick?"

"A Private what?"

"Dick"

"Is being a Dick not something else in English?"

"Yes, it is and sometimes you act like one... just saying." He still wasn't off the hook, but my hard shell was softening, and I could feel myself falling helplessly no matter how hard I tried to resist his magnetic pull.

27

Thursday. The day of the wedding had arrived. Not just the wedding but the big reveal of the return of the stolen Vase of Flowers painting. The atmosphere at the apartment was not like a usual wedding morning at a bride's house. It was far more serene. Brunch was delivered and set up by caterers.

Clive, it turned out, was not just a great motorcycle mechanic, but an award-winning hair stylist, so he popped over and did Ciara's hair.

"Hair styling was what I always wanted to do," he confessed while creating a perfect classic wave through Ciara's silver strands. "But my parents thought it was gay, so I did motorbike mechanics instead. Then after they died, I went back to being the gay man I was born to be. I've also established a name for myself doing drag queen makeup. One of my girls was on the TV show 'RuPaul's Drag Race' do you know it?"

"Not yet. Watching more TV is one of the things I intend to do when I retire next year," I said, longing for days of tranquility with no weddings to plan nor chaos to be fixed.

"I'm here!" Clive's new guy, Davide, arrived in the apartment in a flurry of floral fragrance, carrying the most amazing bo-ho wedding bouquet. The sprays looked like they had just been freshly picked and tied with a silk ribbon, which I knew was not the case. He had created the bouquet style that needed to look perfectly unperfected, which I knew was far more difficult to do than a neat posy. Like naked cakes where the sponge has to be baked and risen enough to achieve the perfect crisp golden tone to be outstanding by itself, as there is no possibility of hiding or disguising an uneven or slightly burnt edge with frosting.

As soon as brunch was over and the caterers had cleared away any evidence, Sophia and I traversed across to the gallery room where the ceremony was to take place. Shadow was given a special permission permit to enter as a guest of honour for uncovering the paintings that all the experts confidently felt were the real deal by Klimt. I didn't want to burst the media's bubble by telling them it was Shadow's love of honey that was the driving force behind the discovery.

The Vase of Flowers painting waited patiently behind red velvet curtains for the unveiling and to be formally welcomed back to its old home.

In a high-security glass showcase in the next room, the Woman with Pearls and Trudie sat behind the disguise of the two Ugly Child portraits, also waiting for their unveiling and be returned to the homes where they belonged. Their unveiling would be slower, as it would take many hours of detailed work by highly skilled art restorers. They were flying in from around the globe to start their magic the following week.

Davide's fresh vase of flowers, which Valentino had given Ciara only days before, sat on a pedestal at the entrance of the room. It had survived well, although Davide had insisted on replacing some of the more delicate stems with fresh ones, when he heard that the international art press were going to present.

The night before, a tipsy Paolo had suggested a dodgy idea to Ciara for decor and she agreed. "It definitely has to happen, please make it happen," she cried, nearly peeing her pants laughing. And it did happened. Two life-size cardboard cutouts of Ugly Child 1 and 2 arrived from a local printer just in time and were positioned on either side of the red velvet curtains. Fresh flower crowns were placed on their heads, made by Davide, and rose petals sprinkled around their feet.

It was the first time a bride would be her own flower girls at one of my weddings, even if they were just cardboard.

The delivery Paolo had been waiting for had also arrived at the security desk. "The stupid courier couldn't find Ciara's address yesterday, so I have told him to deliver the parcel I am waiting for from Rome to the security desk at the studios. Surely he'll be capable of finding the Uffizi?!" Paolo had texted an hour before the ceremony while I met with the PR people for a run through. "Would you mind collecting it and putting it somewhere safe?" So I brought it up to the room with the two ugly children cut outs.

It had been decided that the wedding ceremony would happen first and then the media and other invitees would come into the room for the unveiling. Valentino arrived with Clive, his best man. "Why am I feeling nervous?" he said, wiping his brow with his handkerchief. "I'm 75 years old for goodness' sake."

"Don't worry, it happens to most grooms no matter their age, but it will evaporate as soon as you see your bride, don't worry," I reassured, fixing his boutonniere to his lapel.

"My bride," he laughed, "Gosh, it just struck me again. I'm getting married. At long bloody last!" Clive clapped him on the back. "About time! Let's do this before you back out with nerves."

"No chance," he laughed again as they took their place in front of the red curtain.

As with all my weddings, it started on time. Sophia met Paolo and Ciara at the top of the stairs and I gave the nod to the string quartet to start playing. 'We'll Meet Again'--A fitting love song from the time of World War Two when the painting first disappeared.

The double doors opened to the gallery room and in walked Shadow with a large lavender bow on her neck, followed by Aunt Ciara proudly linked on the arm of her more-handsome-than-ever nephew Paolo. I'm not one for reading romance books, but I'd heard the term 'going weak at the knees' when a guy winked or smiled at the heroine of the story. I brushed it off as codswallop... until now. The wink with his long dark lashes as he walked passed me and the flash of his smile triggered me to grip the door to stop from crumpling on the floor, like the melting witch from Wizard of Oz.

"A museum without its works of art is like a vase without flowers," Valentino paused to choke back a gulp of tears while saying his vows. "We can't say that the Uffizi was empty, but there was something missing, a void. Today a void in the museum is being filled, but a greater void in my life is also being filled. I have spent all my life waiting for that void to be filled. That void being love. You, Ciara, were worth the wait."

I could feel my throat tighten and my eyes pricking. Look up, look away, don't listen. This was my technique at every wedding as I get choked up at them all, even the ones of the bridezillas. I have mastered the art of stopping myself turning into a slobbering mess by looking up, looking away, not listening and focusing on something random. My solution today was to give the Ugly twins a staring match. Of course, they were going to win with their weird cardboard eyes.

Ugly Child number one with her four flecks to illustrate a light shine dancing in her eyes. The dog was the only one with the most normal eyes in the paintings with one fleck, whereas Ugly Child number two had three flecks. Counting the dots was enough distraction to get my stinging eyes under control. All different amounts of light flecks...

that's a weird mistake for a talented artist to make. One, three and four... I tuned back to the vows to hear Ciara saying during hers; "As my mother always said to me, every painting has a secret story to tell." The chatter in my head got louder. One... three, four.

Two... two was missing. Holy crap... Paolo's grandmother had painted code. There was another painting to be found.

28

"Paolo, I think there's another-" I whispered urgently to Paolo standing by my side.

"Shhh," he hushed. He was too busy being emotional to be distracted by me. He was right. It wasn't the appropriate time for me to throw up crack pot ideas. I needed to think about this longer, at least until after the unveiling ceremony and the press had left so that nothing was overheard.

The wedding ceremony guests in the room clapping and the musicians breaking into 'Congratulations' snapped me back into the present. That song was the signal for the gallery's PR people to open the doors, for Sophia and I to shuffle the two cardboard Ugly Children out of sight and for the international media, German and Italian ministers and members of the Looting Committee to enter the room for the unveiling.

Speeches were made, flashes popped, ooohhhs, aaahhhs, gasps, spontaneous clapping erupted as the red curtains were opened and The Vase of Flowers masterpiece was welcomed home.

"I think the painting Raphael did is better, the colours are brighter," muttered Sophia to me behind her hand before joining in the round of applause. After the unveiling, everyone left the room and went to the main hallway where glasses of prosecco were being circulated.

"I'll go on over and help Davide finish setting up the restaurant and take Shadow with me," Sophia said, throwing her long braids behind her shoulders. As there was no real colour theme running through this wedding, she had opted to braid her afro locks to match the colour of the bride and groom's hair; silver and white.

We looked back into the room where Shadow was having her red carpet moment, sitting in front of the painting with Ciara and Valentino on either side with the foreign minister of Germany and an art minister of Italy.

"Okay, I'll get things finished up here. Could you take the two Ugly children with you?" I said casually. A press guest passing overheard and glanced at me in disgust. "Every child is beautiful," they tutted, and had blended into the hive of press being herded down the hallway to the press room before I could explain.

Shadow trotted out and Ciara found a seat against the wall to take a rest on.

"I'll see you two later." I gave Shadow a kiss on the head and blew a kiss to Sophia as they trotted off to the exit sign.

Paolo was chatting with Ciara. "There you are Daisy! That went well, didn't it?"

"Yes, it was beautiful, congratulations." I bent and kissed Ciara's cheek and we exchanged a warm hug.

"Aunt Ciara, I'm dying for you to open the gift I have for you. Did you get it Daisy?"

"I put it under the prosecco table, so it wouldn't be seen."

"Bring it to me and I'll open it now. You have been talking about this surprise so much that I am dying to see it."

Paolo came proudly back with the flat package that looked very like the one that had been be left outside Ciara's apartment by Raphael, but this one was smaller. Ciara tore open the paper open to reveal a large canvas of the head and shoulders of a man with a moustache and beard.

"Another painting, how appropriate!" smiled Ciara.

"Do you recognise him? It's a painting of your father," said Paolo excitedly, unable to wait for her response.

"I recognise him, my dear... but that's not my father. Where did you get it?"

"Grandmother did it. It is your father. I found it stuck in the back of a cupboard when clearing out mother's house when she was moving to the nursing home. Look, there is an inscription on the back on one of the canvas stretchers to my mother. 'For Alice. A portrait of your father. xxx Mama'. I never thought much of it... until you said you hadn't seen a picture of your father in so long. So I think you should have it."

"Paolo, my father never had a beard. He was clean shaven with a small moustache, not a handlebar moustache like this. This painting she did for Alice, your mother... This portrait is of Georgio Ballini. It is just how I remember him."

Silence fell as the three of us gazed on the man that had helped spawn the Ugly Child portraits and given up his life to protect art. But we gazed with confusion lurking in the background. "Paolo," I said slowly, "you told me you shared the same birthday as your mother had, right?"

"Yes, the 21st of August."

"And Ciara, you said your father died around Christmas... after already being away for some months of service?"

"Yes... Oh... ohhh..." Ciara said, her eyes widening, looking at Paolo. "I should have seen it... Paolo. You look very similar to him."

Paolo looked confused. "What, am I missing something?"

"Do the maths!" I said, but not wanting to keep him from the discovery. "Alice–your mother–couldn't have had the same father as Ciara... Your grandfather was Georgio Ballini."

Paolo sat down. "I'm not a Ferrari?"

I sniggered at the statement. "You're not a Volkswagen either." I was being ungracious, considering he had just lost his identity.

"Hmmm," hummed Ciara. "As you are Georgio Ballini's heir, that also makes you a nobleman. You inherit his title as a Marchese."

"Will I now have to curtsy whenever I meet Paolo?" I wished my brain would stop spurting out jokes at such inappropriate times, but it continued. "Raphael will be pleased that nobility has been reinstated in the apartment."

"I don't think titles will matter where he'll be spending the rest of his life when they catch him," snorted Ciara.

Paolo was clearly in shock. "This is insane... I've just gained two new grandfathers in the last hour."

I could see some guests were heading toward Ciara, I needed to get my thoughts out before they got to us "I think there is another painting..."

"We're in the Uffizi there are lots of paintings my dear," laughed Ciara.

"No, I think there must be another Ugly Child painting. Can you remember if your mother painted a third Ugly Child?"

"There's nothing wrong with my memory, dear. My mother did lots of paintings before the war, but the ugly pair are the only ones she did that coincided with the Nazi heist. Unfortunately, if they had not captured Georgio, he would have probably saved a lot more paintings, but after they captured him, and my father was killed in the war that Christmas, she never lifted a paintbrush again. I have a vague recollection of her doing this one. The strong blues and purples in it have triggered the memory... but there were no more ugly children, that is for sure. I despised those two enough. If there was a third I would remember, believe me."

The painting was back in the hands of Paolo as he admired his grandfather's majestic face. If Paolo had a moustache, he would be looking at himself. "I had never paid this painting any attention, but I am seeing this with different eyes now," he said. It suddenly tweaked with me. "Talking of eyes, how many flecks of light in the eyes of your grandfather?"

"What?"

"In the painting... how many flecks of light in his eyes?"

"That's odd. Grandmother really didn't get the basics of painting eyes, did she? When you look closely, there are two in each eye."

"Two? It's it... it's the missing painting," I squeaked.

29

The guests that were walking across in our direction were stalled momentarily, congratulating Valentino.

"Paolo, you could be holding a priceless work of art in your hands," I hushed.

"Another one?" he said anxiously.

I could see pin head droplets forming on his forehead.

"Come on," said Ciara, pushing herself up into standing. "Let me fetch Valentino, we'll make our excuses and quietly slip away to the x-ray room. Cover the painting Paolo, so no one asks any questions."

"Congratul-!" oozed the Italian minister and his wife, who were talking to Valentino, leaning in to kiss Ciara on both cheeks.

"Thank you, but can't talk now. I need my husband for about half an hour..."

The guests looked a little put out that Ciara was not letting them complete their greeting. "To perform husband duties, if you know what I mean..." She gave them a pronounced wink.

Their eyes widened, as did Valentino's. "Natasha," called out Ciara, grabbing Doctor Verbotski's arm as she walked by. "Can you come with us? I need your assistance with... something."

Ciara turned back to the guests, whose expressions were calling for an explanation. "We need all the help we can get in some matters at our age," smiled Ciara.

The Minister cleared his throat, "We'll leave you to it then. I think I need a refill after that," he said to his wife as they walked off.

"What do you have in mind?" asked Valentino, his eyebrows raised.

"We need to go to the x-ray room," whispered Ciara. "We might have found another one."

Valentino glanced down at the rectangular package Paolo had re-wrapped.

"Ohhh... I was getting excited but I'm even more excited now," he said, rubbing his hands together.

Down in the x-ray studio, our little gang gathered. Valentino had texted three other guests, asking them to leave quietly and meet him in the observation room. By the time they had arrived, Valentino, with Natasha's assistance, had the machine on and the painting in place.

Valentino and Ciara sat on two chairs in front of the desk while the rest of us stood behind them. As we glared at the screen an outline became clearer. There *was* a hidden painting.

"My goodness... it can't be..." gasped one of the highbrow experts, nearly falling over as she tried to get closer to the screen.

"It is!" squealed Natasha. It was the first time I heard her monotone voice change, and it was dramatic. "This is like finding the Holy Grail. How exciting!"

The gasps and chatter indicated that everyone recognised what it was except for me and Paolo. I, at last, got the gumption to ask, "What is it?"

All eyes turned to me for a moment. Some had a distinct who-let-her-in look in them.

"It's the Portrait of a Young man by Raphael."

"By Raphael?" Asked Paolo. "Haven't we had enough of his forgeries for one week?" he joked.

"Raphael, the 16th century painter. Not the Raphael with the attic," tutted Ciara, somewhat embarrassed by her nephew's ignorance.

"It is one of the most famous paintings that was stolen for Hitler's Führermuseum," explained Valentino, not letting his eyes move from the screen. "What a day this has turned out to be."

The small room was getting quite hot as word got out and some more of the guests filtered down from the drinks reception.

My phone was buzzing with several "Where are you? We need to start soon," messages from Sophia.

"Oh, crap! Look at the time," I said. "Ciara, Valentino I don't know what you want to do, but we're going to be late for your wedding reception if we don't go soon. Or do you want me to cancel it so you can stay here?"

"No, no," said Ciara. "The Young Man will be here tomorrow and forever more, our wedding day won't be... and besides, I am starving. Let's go." Ciara tapped Valentino on the sleeve, pulling him out of his trance. "Come on husband, we have a wedding cake to cut and a first dance to do."

"If you don't mind, I may skip dinner this evening," said Natasha apologetically, "I would like to get the crew in to work on this."

"Of course," answered Ciara, "we'll save you some cake."

"I do need to ask the question though," said Natasha. "Have you anymore of your mother's paintings?"

"I have all of her paintings, but they are all pre-war landscapes. We can, of course, examine them, but I really think this is the last one Georgio brought to her that day."

Valentino and Ciara left their group of expert friends with slight reluctance, but with a time set to meet and examine the painting again in the morning.

The Gallery PR crew were just leaving at the same time. "Did you get a press goody bag?" asked the PR woman. "We have some left over and it might be a nice keepsake." The tall blonde lady handed me a glossy gift bag. I glanced inside. Information sheets and a guidebook to the Uffizi and a fridge magnet of the Vase of Flowers. "Thank you," I said, "I know a special friend this would be perfect for."

I smiled to myself, thinking of how much Sophia was going to laugh when I presented her with yet another fridge magnet for her collection I constantly added to. All because she once told me how much she hated fridge magnets.

The steps of the Uffizi were lined with pop-up artists. Some were selling finished works of art, others offering portraits and caricatures, others were lost in their sketch pads and easels, filling their canvases with the beauty of Florence before them. A mime artist of Michelangelo's ghost was packing up for the day.

Paolo and I strolled behind the newlyweds. Ciara proudly linked arms with her new husband as we walked towards Piazza della Signoria, soaking up the sense of relaxation that Florence always seemed to emit rather than the anxiety-filled chaos that other cities filled me with.

"I've had enough excitement this week to last me another lifetime," chuckled Ciara, turning onto the street where the warm welcoming glow of the restaurant shone halfway down. "Honestly, what a day this has turned out to be."

"It's not over yet," I mumbled to Paolo as I nodded towards the figure standing near the restaurant's facade. "Did you invite him?"

Waiting for us was Detective Emanuele. "No, of course not, he must have some news."

My mind flicked immediately to the fingerprints on the murder weapon. What if they were Valentinos...

30

"Good evening, I'm sorry to disturb you all on this special day," said Detective Marella coyly. He wasn't brandishing any handcuffs, so that was a relief.

Sophia came out of the restaurant door at that moment. "There you are! We thought we would have to start without you!"

"Sorry for the delay Sophia, we will be in, in a moment. Detective Emanuele needs a quick word." said Valentino, emphasising the word quick as his stomach audibly protested another delay.

"I thought you'd want to hear that Raphael's car has been found... by a cliff," Detective Marella stated. "He left a note. I thought you should read it Signora Ciara."

On the front of the opened envelop was written: 'Please hand deliver to the Police Station in Florence Centre.'

Ciara handed the envelop to Paolo, who unfolded the parchment paper inside and read it aloud.

To Whom It Concerns:

I, master artist, Raphael Corbo of Florence, killed Julia Svoboda in the early hours of last Sunday morning. I have taken my own life as I can't live with myself after what I have done. It was a crime of passion, passion for art.

With the Vase of Flowers, I had created the perfect reproduction. I created it so that people could have enjoyed the work of art and be soothed that it had been found. Isotopes or no isotopes, now that the original is back, I am sure you will agree that mine is the better version.

"How insolent of him," said Ciara, drowning out Sophia's same time comment to me of; "Isn't that what I said?"

Paolo went on:

This is not the first time I have done this. There are two perfect reproductions by me in the Vatican museums, but no one has ever found them. Crowds gather and admire them, get lost in them. I have often gone there just to watch people marvel at my paintings. Why does it matter what name is on them?—they are magnificent. My paintings are admired and loved and that will be my legacy.

'I knew there was no risk of the original of the Lady with Pearls being found, because I have it. It may take you a while to find it in my apartment. Hidden by a child all this time. That is the only clue I am giving.'

"He was more the fool for thinking we wouldn't find it," interrupted Valentino.

Shadow let a loud whimper. "Sorry that a clever dog wouldn't find it."

I had planned a way for this masterpiece to be discovered and I have no doubt it would pass as the original work by Klimt. (Again I would like to argue the point, does it matter who painted the work of art when the pieces are identical and crafted by masters of equal talent?)

Julia had overheard what Filippo and I were doing. Julia told me she had found a buyer in Dubai, and insisted I sell it as the original and give her half, or she would expose me.

I was not doing the painting for the money; I was doing it for the art and improvement on what went before. I wanted it to hang in the Uffizi so that people could admire it, for my work to be where it should, amongst the greats.

Like the Vase of Flowers, my Woman with Pearls was more than perfect, better than the original, for sure. Isn't that what life is about, to improve things, to strive towards flawless perfection? I just wanted to bring joy through art and someday be known as the artist that bettered the greats. We were so close, and she was going to ruin it. That is why I did it. I had to silence her.

Anna's pottery wire had broken, and she needed another. I had gone to get one from the studio. Filippo was just doing a check on my final piece with Julia. It was after he left that Julia told me her demands. Neither Anna nor Filippo played any part in the silencing.

I regret what I did to Julia, but more so I regret immensely that my years of work will never be appreciated.

In this envelope, I have included a letter for Anna. Please give it to her sealed and respect the private contents.

I bid you all and this harsh world farewell.

Raphael Corbo

Master Artist.

"I am sorry for Anna's loss, but what an arrogant, egotistical git he was to think he could improve on the work of greats by forging their art," said Valentino.

"Now Detective Emanuele, if that is it, I would like to bring my wife in for dinner. We are both tired from such an overwhelming day. You are welcome to join us if you would like?"

"Thank you for the offer," said Emanuele. "But I need to be getting back to the station. We have sent on the closed letter to Anna. She has gone to her family in the Czech Republic. I wish you both well and many years of happiness together."

He tipped his head and walked off into the now darkening streets, making the glow of warm light from the restaurant all the more welcoming.

Over dinner Raphael, of course, became the focus of conversation on the top table between Sophia, the newlyweds, myself and Paolo. "But if he just wanted people to enjoy the work of art, why didn't he just hand over the original when he discovered it?" asked Sophia.

"It takes a lot of skill and work to clean paint from an overlaid painting. He had access to the x-ray facilities, but he didn't have the restoration skills needed," explained Valentino. "Although Ciara's mother knew what she was doing and used gentle homemade pigments, that seems it will be quite easy to remove without damaging the works of art."

"You should give Shadow the job of removing the paint," I said, finishing the first course.

"But that doesn't answer my question," said Sophia. "Why didn't he just hand it over to be professionally cleaned?"

"Ego," chipped in Paolo. "He wanted his version to be the one hanging in the Uffizi. Even though it was plagiarism, he didn't seem to see it that way. He probably would have let it slip at some point, people like that can't keep that kind of secret to themselves. Let's hope he let it slip to someone about which forgeries are his that hang in the Vatican otherwise they will be years trying to identify which ones. There are so many works of art in the Vatican it will take them an age to find them."

"Seventy thousand works of art, actually. I learned that from a priest called Father Dan on my last visit to the Vatican City, you may remember him..." I winked at Paolo. "But it won't take that long... they should be easy to find now. Raphael's ego just gave all the clues needed."

"What clues?" silence fell on the table. Paolo filled up my wineglass as if that was a way to encourage my tongue to be loosened.

"Well, he had not perfected faces at that point, so the forgeries are paintings that he did some time ago before he could do faces. So we are looking for paintings without faces in them, that should eliminate quite a lot of the religious works. But the biggest clue is Raphael himself."

I took a sip of my wine and leaned back in my chair, crossing my legs, basking in their expressions, as if they were waiting for the last kick in a penalty shootout at a World Cup football final.

"All they need to do is identify dates Raphael was at the museum and find him on CCTV. He says he would watch people looking at his paintings, so it will be the paintings you find him on CCTV spending time observing people at."

The silence was deadly before Valentino picked his chin up. I took another sip of wine. "You're a genius! A total genius!... A Toast to Daisy the Genius." As everyone around the table clinked their glasses to the chorus of "To Daisy the Genius!" Paolo squeezed my leg.

"I've never dated a genius before."

"You still haven't. We are not dating, remember?"

"Oh, come on, is this not a date?"

"No, it's a wedding I organised for your aunt at high speed after you duped me into coming to her 80th birthday so you wouldn't look like a lonely ass without a partner."

"I was hoping you wouldn't find me out."

"I'm a genius, remember?"

"So where does a man bring a genius on a date when he asks her out?"

"That's for you to figure out. But for now, don't push your luck," I winked.

————

You are invited to Castello Trasimeno, Umbria, Italy
For the bachelorette party of Rachel Kevins
We asked for a murder mystery party but the wedding planner seemed
hesitant due to 'her past reputation'? Anyway be prepared for lots of wine
and a mystery treasure hunt. We are taking over the castle so we hope at
least one knight in shining armour will arrive!

They get what they asked for ... they never stated the knight should
be living.
You can order 'A Deathly Wedding Knight'
Book 3 in The Deadly Wedding Cozy Mystery Series
through Rosie Meleady's Amazon Page.

————

READER FREE BONUS!

If you would like to read the private letter Raphael wrote to Anna and Anna's response to the detective who sent it on to her go to: http://rosiemeleady.com/index.php/annas-letter/

***

AFTERWORD

Author End Notes:

I love mixing some Italian experiences and history in my mysteries and love including new gems of information that I find during my research. However, I just want to clarify fact and fiction:

There is no painting by Klimt called the Woman with Pearls. I created this for the sake of the story. However, there were 6,000 works of art and cultural pieces looted by the Nazis, including The Vase of Flowers, which was returned to the Uffizi in 2019. Many works of art are still missing. This includes the Portrait of Trudie by Gustav Klimt and The Portrait of a Young Man by Raphael.

The Portrait of Trudie was commissioned around 1900 before Klimt became a very prominent painter throughout Vienna. Jenny Steiner commissioned the painting after her daughter had died and the painting depicts Trudie at 13 years old.

Jenny Steiner fled Austria in 1938 shortly after the Nazi invasion of Vienna. The Nazis took the painting that same year, under the pretence of being part of a collection to pay taxes. It was sold at auction around April 1941 to a mysterious buyer. The painting hasn't been seen since.

The Portrait of a Young Man by the Italian High Renaissance artist, Raphael, was stolen during World War II. Initially, the property of the Polish noble family, Czartoryski, the painting was one of the many taken by the Nazis during Hitler's rule. This painting was confiscated by one of Hitler's senior officials, Hans Frank, who took it for Hitler's Führermuseum. The painting was last seen in Frank's residence in 1945 and it has been missing ever since.

Perhaps it is time to check your attic or look a little closer at any paintings of ugly children in your home?

I based Valentino's vows on the words of Germany's foreign minister, Heiko Maas, who backed Italy's efforts to retrieve the Vase of Flowers from the heirs of the soldier who took it. He said these words on the 19th July 2019 when The Vase of Flowers was unveiled at the Uffizi: "A museum without its works of art is like a vase without flowers. We can't say that the Uffizi was empty, but there was something missing, a void. Today we are here to fill that void."

ABOUT THE AUTHOR

Dubliner Rosie Meleady has been a magazine publisher and editor since 1994. She won the International Women in Publishing Award 1996 at the ripe old age of 24. She couldn't attend the award ceremony in London as she decided it would also be a good day to give birth. Her favourite board game growing up was Cluedo, and as an adult she started a Missing Persons Agency.

In her 'A Rosie Life In Italy' series, she writes about buying a 22 roomed derelict villa in Italy by accident, renovating it and existing in Italy.

Her love of solving mysteries led her to start writing her 'Deadly Wedding Cozy Mystery' series. She now lives happily ever after in Italy disguised as a wedding planner, while renovating the villa and writing long into the night.

Follow Rosie on her blog and social media:

www.rosiemeleady.com